They strolled through the Gamla Stan, Stockholm's Old Town, with its cobblestone alleys and buildings of muted colors and carved wood. The air was filled with brisk flurries of snow.

One minute they were walking forward, continuing to talk about spa operations, and then, really not meaning to, really, Jackson took Esme's hand. Her skin was unspeakably silky. He shot his eyes over to her for approval. She looked down at their entwined hands, as surprised as he was, like a force in and of itself had made the move, neither of them having anything to do with it. The thing was, it felt absolutely natural, normal and right. As if their hands had been searching for each other's since the beginning of time. Like they had each been lost and finally found their way home.

A peace came across his face, another move happening without him consciously instructing it to. He stopped walking, which pulled her a little closer to him. Still holding one hand, he took hold of the other. And when his face drew just a few inches from hers, he kissed her.

Dear Reader,

Prior to writing stories of romance and love, I was a journalist. One of the sectors I wrote for was well-being. Through that, I was introduced to the world of spa. I've been wanting to incorporate what I learned about that centuries-old tradition into a story of two people who need self-care and each other. Meet spa professional Esme and naysayer Jackson. He initially thinks that spas are merely a luxury for the privileged. She changes his mind on a whirlwind adventure from New York to spas in Sweden, Mexico and Thailand, where they discover love along the way.

Since wellness is at the forefront of their story, I thought I'd suggest a few techniques you can do at home to take care of yourself, something we often neglect.

Soak a smooth stone in hot water to a comfortable temperature. Use it in a circular motion as a massage tool on a sore or tight spot.

Lie down on your back and place a tennis ball under your neck. Rotate your head up and down and side to side.

Nourish your hair and scalp by massaging with ordinary coconut oil. After an hour, rinse and shampoo.

Enjoy Esme and Jackson's story.

Love,
Andrea x

JET-SET ESCAPE WITH HER BILLIONAIRE BOSS

ANDREA BOLTER

Harlequin

ROMANCE

Harlequin®
ROMANCE

ISBN-13: 978-1-335-21606-9

Jet-Set Escape with Her Billionaire Boss

Harlequin Enterprises ULC
22 Adelaide St. West, 41st Floor
Toronto, Ontario M5H 4E3, Canada
www.Harlequin.com

Printed in U.S.A.

Recycling programs for this product may not exist in your area.

Andrea Bolter has always been fascinated by matters of the heart. In fact, she's the one her girlfriends turn to for advice with their love lives. A city mouse, she lives in Los Angeles with her husband and daughter. She loves travel, rock 'n' roll, sitting at cafés and watching romantic comedies she's already seen a hundred times. Say hi at andreabolter.com.

Books by Andrea Bolter

Harlequin Romance

Billion-Dollar Matches collection

Caribbean Nights with the Tycoon

Her Las Vegas Wedding
The Italian's Runaway Princess
The Prince's Cinderella
His Convenient New York Bride
Captivated by Her Parisian Billionaire
Wedding Date with the Billionaire
Adventure with a Secret Prince
Pretend Honeymoon with the Best Man

Visit the Author Profile page at Harlequin.com.

For my BAND group

Praise for
Andrea Bolter

CHAPTER ONE

"YOU NEED TO learn to relax, Jackson." Dr. Singh leaned forward in his chair, obviously trying to make his point. "When was the last time you took a vacation? Or walked on the beach, or even played a round of golf?"

"There are only so many hours in a day," Jackson quipped after pausing to reach into his pocket and tilt up his phone screen so he could get a quick check of the time. After his examination, Dr. Singh had asked him to step into his cluttered office, where they sat across each other at his desk. Jackson was already behind schedule, the doctor visit taking longer than he'd anticipated. "I'm swamped." Indeed, running the acquisitions company that became his after his parents died took every moment from him. Who had time for a vacation?

"Being busy doesn't exempt you from taking care of yourself."

With both of his parents dying much younger than average age, Jackson was screened regularly in the hope that any developing heath problem would be caught and treated early. But he'd scheduled a special appointment because the tightness in his neck and shoulders was becoming more frequent.

"I felt that muscle strain you're talking about. You're hard as a rock. You report headaches in addition to the occasional shortness of breath. Those are irregularities in a thirty-three-year-old man. We'll run some tests but I think what you're describing is chronically uncontrolled stress."

Jackson figured plenty of people lived to ripe old ages with lives that didn't leave time for golf. He tried to speed up the conversation with a short "Fine." At least Dr. Singh didn't think he was in immediate danger.

"I'm serious. It's long thought that lifestyle, and mental and spiritual wellness, greatly influence health. You need to rest, eat well, exercise. And take breaks from all of it every once in a while. Did your parents have pursuits other than work?"

"Are you kidding?" Jackson snarked. He

thought back to his father and mother when he was growing up, both putting in eighteen-hour days, sometimes seven days a week like he did now. His doctor was stating the obvious, that Jackson was following in their footsteps. Which he knew in his gut to be true.

Still, the Finns weren't people with hobbies or sports or pastimes. They worked a lot and slept a little, plain and simple. That's how empires were built and maintained. Jackson's lean physique was the result of poorly digested meals eaten indifferently at desks and on airplanes more than from following a nutrition strategy.

"I think it's essential that you make some changes. Carve out the time for yourself. You must find a balance or you're going to get sick. How about starting with a massage? That can be restorative."

Dr. Singh had no idea how ironic his suggestion was.

One, two, three, four, five stories, Jackson counted, eyes ticking upward as he studied the Sherwood Building across the street from where the driver dropped him off after his doctor's appointment. He owned that historic building, or that was to say that Finn Enterprises did. Which, of course, now came to mean Jackson and Jackson alone, as he was an only child. With his mother's untimely death followed by his father's, he was left with full ownership of their many assets. He hadn't seen the landmark Sherwood Building in a year, so long ago that while he knew it was five floors, he wanted to get a good view of the structure from across the street, counting the stories to reconfirm. He'd be spending time here now, remembered agonies notwithstanding. Jackson was on a mission.

New York's busy Tribeca neighborhood surrounded him. A syllabic abbreviation for Triangle Below Canal Street, the Lower Manhattan neighborhood was renowned. In the early eighteen hundreds the area's Washington Market was a central shopping hub for meat and fish, dairy and produce. In fact, upon completion in 1830, the Sherwood Building itself held dry goods merchants. By the end of that century many of the area's original brick buildings were replaced by factories, manufacturers and warehouses. Fortunately, the lovingly nicknamed Sher survived. In the past fifty or so years, Tribeca received a huge boon when filmmakers, artists and celebrities began buying up property. Now a mélange of restoration, new construction, green spaces and a few remaining cobblestoned streets, it was one of the city's most unique enclaves.

Even with the typical New York swirl of hurried pedestrians, horns honking and the rattle of subways underground, Jackson's eyes stayed glued to his building. He'd really forgotten how dramatic it was, Italianate architecture with huge arched windows on the street level, and cast-iron front facades that were among the first of their kind in New York. He was proud to be such a grand old dame's owner.

On the street, businesses populated every available space. A boba café stood on one side of the Sher with a pet groomer on the other. The building's ground floor was leased to an art dealer and a couple of colorful abstract paintings hung in those front windows. Offices on the second, third and fourth floors housed longtime tenants. It was the fifth, and top, floor where Jackson had business today.

Some of those memories he dreaded ticked across his mind like a camera roll of still photographs. His awful debacle of a marriage had nearly shut down operations four years ago on the fateful fifth floor, which housed a day spa that had previously made every best-of list around the globe. Until Jackson's disaster. After that, it languished. Operational but underutilized. No longer buzzed about, true spa aficionados having long moved on to newer places. With a swallow, Jackson reaffirmed to himself that he was going to restore Spa at the Sher to the greatness it once held a reputation for. It was the least he could do for his parents. They wouldn't be there to see it, but Jackson would know he did it.

It was actually a paradox that the Finns owned a spa at all, given their all-work-and-no-play mode of operation, as Dr. Singh had just pointed out. It was only one business within their varied portfolio, but obtaining a landmark building in Manhattan was, in and of itself, a crowning triumph for his parents. Starting from an early age, they'd both worked three jobs a day to save up enough money to leave Ohio and start a life in New York. That they made it to the top, to own one of the city's most famous addresses, was truly an American dream. Jackson turned it into a nightmare.

It gnawed him alive that he had let their

prized acquisition become irrelevant because of bad decisions. Meanwhile, other luxury spas pressed forward with beautiful designs and features, and both classic and cutting-edge offerings. With no new innovations, the Sher had lost its luster. Jackson himself had been isolating and living in hotels everywhere but New York, as if avoiding the city would make all the history fade away. Now he was finally back, as the spa's group of investors was gathering in a few weeks to vote on the fate of Spa at the Sher.

The spa deserved to be restored to its former glory, and Jackson was going to convince the investors of such. Lest they vote to back out of their shares in the business. He'd get rid of that cute fairy they'd hired as manager who they'd never given any power to. What was her name—Emma, Eden, Elsa? He'd hire a real spa director with a vision and give him or her the budget to implement it. Hopefully then the ache in the back of his neck that represented the past would subside. And perhaps he wouldn't wake up unable to catch his breath in dark hotel rooms alone in the middle of the night anymore.

Maybe he'd even take his doctor's advice and get a massage. After all, that was one of the services spas were best known for. There was a time when Spa at the Sher employed some of the best massage therapists on the planet, who came with their own client rosters and weeks-long waiting lists. He'd return it to those good old days.

He took in the majesty of the Sher one more time before retrieving that pixie girl's name from his phone. Up in the window of the fifth floor, part of the spa, Jackson spotted someone gazing down to the street scene. It looked like a woman. Was it that manager? For some unexplainable reason, a wiggle shot up his spine.

"My six-o'clock glycolic-acid-peel client canceled so I'm going home," Demi, one of the Spa at the Sher's estheticians, said to Esme, who was gazing down to the street from the large fifth-floor windows.

"Okay, see you tomorrow," she answered without turning. She didn't know why she was gazing down from the windows or what she was looking for. Well, actually she did. But she had things to do, so, with great effort, pulled herself away. She returned to her tasks, separating a large vase of colorful flowers into smaller ones so that she could place them on three different tables in the reception area. *He* was expected any minute now and she wanted to make the spa shine as much as it could.

After all, although the spa had no director, and therefore no direction, as manager she was running things with what she had to work with. Right down to repurposing a floral arrangement, or buying some new flavors of tea for clients to enjoy. Anything she could do so that guests had a memorable experience and would return. At that thought, she clicked her tongue against the roof of her mouth. *Not easy.* Not when there were incredible, unforgettable spas all over the world that offered so much more than the stodgy old Sher, which had seen better days.

"The Vichy shower is broken again," Esme's assistant manager, Trevor, announced as he came out from the main corridor and into the reception area. "Do you want me to call for repair?"

"Yeah. Get them to come as soon as they can. I don't want to have to rebook anyone because of it."

Trevor turned and ducked into a treatment room. Esme neatened up the front desk, putting away the sticky notes staff sometimes left for each other reminding them of things that needed doing. She didn't know why she was nervous. Maybe it was because owner Jackson Finn hadn't said why he was coming in as opposed to the typical email or phone call that was his usual method of communication. He rarely even scheduled a video meeting. Appearing after what Esme guessed was close to a year made no sense. Unless he was coming to fire her, having the decency to at least do that in person.

She again peered down to the street, as if she would recognize him in the crowd at this distance. When she'd seen him on video and a few times in person, she did notice how handsome he was, with his thick dark hair, impeccable in tailored business clothes and a devastating smile that made rare appearances. All of that was neither here nor there, merely observation. She reassured herself that he had no grounds to fire her. The spa wasn't losing money; they were afloat. It had lost its charm, though it was a perfectly serviceable establishment. The Wall Street crowd did still make their way up for deep tissue massages, sometimes booked at regular biweekly intervals to fit in with busy schedules. The Tribeca and SoHo art scene still trickled in for the ministrations given to battle the damaging effects of big city life. The Sher was still as much a part of the neighborhood as the dry cleaners and the pizzeria.

Esme remembered years ago reading about it in spa magazines. The historic building. The fifth-floor oasis of pampering and unfathomable luxury in Lower Manhattan. She'd read interviews with the professionals who worked here and had brought leading-edge everything from the online accounting program to the latest in skin rejuvenation. They'd all moved on now. Esme didn't know the full story of why the spa had fallen from its highest peak. When she was brought in four years ago, she'd heard gossip that Jackson's wife had been running things. Or that was to say, ruining things. Esme was curious about what really transpired but was never privy to anything other than hearsay.

Doing her final walk-through before he was to make his return, she double-checked the side table that displayed those new teas. One large clear cylinder held cool water infused with cucumber and a second one was flavored with lemon slices. There were whole fresh fruits, nuts and dark chocolate to nibble.

With its palate of the palest lavender and sage accents against tan furniture, it was welcoming, pleasant although dated. All of the walls held photos, paintings or drawings of flowers. Again, pretty but not compelling. Likewise, the treatment menu itself was flat, nothing to offer those chasing the next new experience. There was nothing she could do to dazzle Jackson. A spa without a director, a direction and a budget to make it happen was stagnant.

Hearing the elevator doors open outside the spa's glass entrance door and catching sight of tall and formidable Jackson Finn meant that she was about to find out what brought him in. He opened the heavy door and entered, his dark brown eyes quickly scanning the foyer until they landed on her. "Esme Russo, right?"

"Are you okay?" Ooh, that was a bit personal but it popped out of her mouth. His shoulders were practically touching his ears, obvious even under the bulk of his fine wool coat.

"What?"

"Your shoulders are so tense."

"Yeah, I know. Everybody keeps telling me that."

He approached and reached out his hand to shake hers. Which was strange to her. Spa people didn't shake hands. If you knew someone, you hugged and if you didn't, you weren't sure how they felt about touch so wouldn't want to invade their personal space until that was established. In any case, she'd forgotten that Jackson had a formality about him that was instantly out of place at the spa. Out of propriety she returned the handshake. His was firm and his hand all but wrapped around hers, an unexpectedly pleasant sensation.

"Can I take your coat?"

As he removed the garment topping a formal gray suit and handed it to her, she had this ridiculous impulse to bring it to her nose just to see what his smell was like. Of course, she resisted and quickly shook her head in surprise at herself. She hung the coat on the rack put out in the colder months so that clients weren't encumbered with heavy outerwear they didn't need in the warmth of the spa. When she turned around she saw that his eyes were directed at her, and she had the sense that he'd been watching every move she made. Please, please, please. Don't let him have come to fire her. With her considerable experience, it wouldn't be hard for her to find another job, but being fired never looked good on a résumé.

Jackson then scrutinized the reception area. Two sofas and the registration desk, with the relaxation room in sight to the right. "Was this how the front room was arranged last time I was here?"

Oh, no. She was sure she heard disapproval in his voice. "I believe so. We may have repositioned the sofas with a bit more feng shui."

He raised his eyebrows as if he didn't understand her. Was it possible he didn't know what feng shui was? She supposed, as the CEO of a multi-million-dollar company, he had underlings that handled everything for him including the harmony of environment. "Were you successful?" He caught her eyes so they locked with his. Wow, they were deep and soulful, brown like black coffee. She also saw pain inside them, and not just from the stiffness of the shoulders.

"Successful in what?"

"Improving the feng shui."

"I don't know if that's really measurable. It's just a flow decision."

"A flow decision?" Why did his tone sound like an interrogation?

After all, if he wasn't going to be involved with the spa enough to see it more than once a year, he didn't really get to be critical. Moving a couple of sofas around to create a more welcoming entry didn't seem like a change so big that she even needed to communicate it to her higher-ups. "Do you dislike it?"

He shrugged those stiff, broad shoulders slightly. "I don't have a feeling about it one way or the other." He was so tightly wound. He obviously didn't lead a spa lifestyle. Peering over to the beverage table in the relaxation room, he asked, "Are those cucumber slices in the water?"

"Yes."

"Your clients enjoy that?" Again he sounded like he had either just landed from another planet or thought she had.

Without waiting, she dashed over to pour him a glassful. "Try it. It's very refreshing."

He eyed it skeptically before taking a sip. Again she felt like her entire career now rested in that eight ounces of water as he weighed his decision. "Blech."

Failure! As if she'd just lost a contest.

Surprisingly though, he tried a second

time. When he brought his full lips to the rim of the cup, she nervously licked her own. How did he make the act of drinking a beverage seem so…important? He didn't appear to like the water any more on the second sip.

"Would you like to sit down?"

"No."

"Is there something I could do for you, then?" She still had no idea what the true purpose of his visit was, and whether she was to assist him with it in some way.

He pointed to the computer at the reception desk. "Who has access here to your system?"

Wasn't that an obvious answer? "Staff."

"All of them?" What was he fishing for?

"Pardon me, I mean the administrative staff. Myself, my assistant manager, Trevor, and our two front desk supervisors."

"How often do you change access passwords?"

"I believe it's on our schedule every six months."

"It's very important." Esme thought he sounded suspicious. She felt a bit insulted by that. Maybe it was an attitude left over from what she'd heard were some shady dealings at the spa before she'd started working here. "I'd like to refamiliarize myself with the space."

She couldn't ask why. All she could get out was, "Okay. A couple of the treatment rooms are in use—" she pointed down the corridor "—but otherwise, I'm sure you know your way around."

"Actually, I don't really remember the lay-out."

That was so unexpected she had to collect herself with a deep inhale through her nose and a slow exhale through her mouth. She hadn't realized she'd be giving Jackson Finn a tour of his own property.

CHAPTER TWO

JACKSON DIDN'T DOUBT that there were people in the world, New Yorkers even, who enjoyed a glass of water with mushy chunks of bitter plants in it. He just wasn't one of them and wondered what it would take to get that godawful taste out of his mouth. Perhaps a pastry from the Italian café down the block. Fortunately, there was a bowl of mints on one of the tables so he could grab a couple and pop them into his mouth immediately, which made an instant improvement.

"If you'll follow me, then." Esme pointed to the main corridor. He'd forgotten how pretty she was. She wore brown trousers topped by a sweater that was woven in varying shades of pink. Somehow the pink and brown complemented each other in a most unlikely combo that was unusual and upbeat at the same time. She no longer had what he'd thought of as a short pixie haircut; instead the brown locks had grown into a choppy shag with golden highlights that brushed her shoulders.

The sweater ended at her hip, and when she turned and gestured for him to follow, her most attractive behind swung a bit under the fabric of the trousers. Jackson checked himself. He was hardly in the habit of perusing women's bodies. Since his divorce four years ago he'd had intimate encounters with women, business types he met in bars around the world, when his mortal need for human contact had reached a crucial proportion and he had to have a release. The women were picked by their ability to understand that was all he was available for. He was exactly one and done when it came to relationships after the horror show known as Livia.

It was interesting that even Esme had noticed his shoulders were tight. Apparently, it was that obvious. Tension had become his normal state. Once he got the spa revamp underway, would all that he'd submerged release? He knew Dr. Singh was right that if he didn't manage his stress and modify his lifestyle he was surely on his way to the same early grave as his parents. Though in the past he'd dismissed advice to slow down and find ways to recharge, he acknowledged to himself that it had now become critical.

"This is typical of our massage suites." Esme pushed open a door to let Jackson enter. The room had the same cordial, if drab, decor as the reception area, referencing flowers as decoration. Dried stems in a collection of small vases adorned the side table while black-and-white photos of various blooms were hung four in a row on the wall. Meditation-type music played at a low volume. Regarding the massage table in the center of the room, she informed him, "We use Northstar tables in all of the suites. I think they're the best on the market. Made with a high-density foam that lasts a lot longer than some of the other brands."

"I wouldn't know. I rarely use spa services." Her eyebrows bunched. "Interesting that you own one, then, isn't it?" He was taken aback—or was it intrigued?—by her bluntness yet it was something he'd asked himself. In his family, self-indulgence was not part of the regime. The Finns toiled; that's what they did. Spa was foreign to them other than profit/loss statements. Esme bringing it up merely added to the ludicrousness of the situation.

"My parents bought the Sher for its status as a landmark building. The spa was already established here so we figured we'd just continue with it. That is to say until my wife, my ex-wife, my then-wife..." Jackson tripped over his words. He still felt pure shame that he'd let any facet of this historic building into the hands of flinty Livia, who not only falsified business records for her own financial gain, but also cheated on Jackson with a man she organized the whole scheme with. His parents were furious at their son's lack of judgment in a partner.

Livia wasn't at all the type they'd have wanted him to couple off with in the first place. They were serious people. Never a couple. Never romantic. Never displaying love. Livia was loud and dramatic and liked the sound of her own voice. Jackson was attracted to the flash and fantasy, if only to offset what felt like an emptiness in the somber life he'd grown up in. His parents couldn't understand any more than Jackson could, really, why he was cut from a different cloth and needed more than the life they had created. He became enraptured, which led him to trust her, and that's how the trouble began. After the fury from the embezzlement, Jackson sensed a pervasive malaise grow in his parents, a disappointment in their son that he believed contributed to their untimely deaths, a stabbing guilt that he still carried. Which was why he returned. He couldn't bring them back to life but he could the spa.

Esme was probably completely unaware of the Finn family's problems when she was hired. He'd put his human resources team right to work finding a replacement for his cheating ex-wife, who he fired as soon as her ruse was discovered by a thankfully persistent accountant. They decided to bring in a manager, rather than a director. Someone who could just keep things running while they figured out what to do next. His HR people had picked Esme's résumé from a stack of others.

Unfortunately, Jackson's interest in the spa languished alongside his parents' weariness and their deaths. So much time had passed that his investors recently informed him they were considering pulling out of the partnership. The news lit a fire in Jackson he didn't know he could kindle. It was now or never for him to rebuild the spa's relevance or sell it off. Unfinished business whose time had come.

"It's an exquisite building."

Esme stopped his ruminating on Livia and those awful times. "Do you like it here?"

"Um, sure." She seemed thrown by the question and didn't know how to answer. He wondered if that meant that she didn't. Not an easy thing to say to the owner, especially not knowing him well.

She led him into another treatment room set up for facial work. "Here's one of our skin care rooms. We've got a separate sound system in each room—" she pointed to the speakers in each corner "—if the client likes particular music. We also utilize candles and aromatherapy."

"Is that what I'm smelling?" Jackson sniffed.

"That's actually the product we use in our pineapple facial."

"You use pineapple in the treatment?"

"It's the key ingredient in the products we use for the protocol. Pineapple contains a powerful enzyme, bromelain, that's great for the face."

"Pineapple. On someone's face. Not on a fruit plate." He didn't know why he was trying a little humor. Maybe because he was so out of place. All he knew about skin care was that he had to put sunscreen on after he shaved. "Why would anyone want to smell like fruit?"

She smiled, which he was glad for.

"I guess that might seem strange but in this case, it has a purpose. Scent can also be unwinding or stimulating, depending on what we're going for. A favorite smell can be transformative to the client during the fifty minutes or so that they're in the treatment room with us."

Jackson remembered how his doctor told him that he needed to find ways to relax. Although he couldn't imagine mucky cucumber water and sickly sweet smells as getting that done for him. He absentmindedly rubbed the back of his neck.

"May I ask, are you having some distress? I noticed your shoulders were tense when you came in. And just now I saw you self-massaging your neck."

He hadn't realized that he'd brought his hand behind his neck or that the motion had a name. "No. I'm not here for a massage." Despite whether or not he needed one. Esme's spine stiffened at the harshness of his tone. He hadn't meant to offend her. "Carry on."

He followed her farther down the corridor. "This is our wet room." It was as if the entire room she showed him was one gigantic shower, with floor-to-ceiling tiling, a large treatment bed in the center that had some sort of drainage below and a contraption above it that had seven water jets.

He had a vague recollection of receiving a very large plumbing bill to repair some sort of problem in this room. "What is this?"

"It's called a Vichy shower. The jets rain down on the client and we adjust the temperature and the water pressure to create a massage-like experience. Unfortunately, it's on the fritz yet again." Esme certainly knew what she was talking about, unlike him. After getting rid of Livia, he found less emotionally fraught projects to concentrate on. But it ate into his gut as a physical manifestation of letting his parents down. He wasn't born to a happy and demonstratively loving family. But his parents were good people and he discredited them by thinking he had to have the swirl of romance they considered a waste of time.

Esme continued her tour with the men's

shower and locker room. "We've got a large whirlpool bathtub, steam room, six showers, two vanity areas and full-length cedar lockers. Another snack lounge, complimentary toiletries, hair dryers, lots of charging stations. I love our guests to stay for a lengthy visit with us, and take as much of a break from the real world as they can spare. And leave rejuvenated."

Rejuvenated. Interesting. Though he'd never thought of a spa that way. That it could become a personal oasis, a fee-paying club of sorts. He'd categorized it as a luxury for people with cash to burn, not unlike money spent on jewelry or expensive restaurants. When his parents bought the spa, there had been a longtime management team who'd spent over twenty years creating a top-notch, highly regarded establishment.

When the Finns bought it, that group took the change of ownership as an opportunity to move on, opening a few spas of their own in the Midwest. Then Livia came along implementing changes that didn't work, and willy-nilly eliminations of services that clients still actually wanted. Plus, in retrospect, even Livia's high-strung, reedy voice and fast, jerky way of moving never matched with what was supposed to be the vibe of the spa. Unlike Esme, whose lush voice sounded like the middle of a cool forest. One that he could walk through and feel a grounding he'd never even imagined. There was something unique about her.

He asked her solely because it popped into his head, "Where did you work before you joined us?" Obviously, he could have gotten that information from a résumé they must have had on file and she probably thought it was ridiculous that he hadn't. Or she might be wondering why he was inquiring after she'd already been working at the Sher for four years.

Nonetheless she responded, giving him the chance to hear her thick, luscious speaking voice again. "I held a supervisory position at a luxury hotel spa in Miami. Prior to that I spent two years at a Mayan spa in Mexico. And before that I did an apprenticeship in Denmark."

"So, you're not a stranger to moving around."

"Actually, I was born and raised in New York. In the Bronx. I can't think of anywhere I'd rather settle. New York is in my blood."

He let a smile tip up. He was raised in New York, too, although far from the Bronx.

He grew up on Long Island in the wealthy suburbs. After Livia, New York was nothing but streets of regret so he stayed away. Although lately he'd been thinking otherwise. How long could he run, remaining a nomad of cold hotels and no roots?

The Sher's physical space was terrific; it was the lack of vision and keeping up to date that was needed. Weeks of work, not months, would be all that was required.

A couple of dangling pieces clicked into his mind. How much a spa director and a spa manager were different. He'd want a director who knew spas all over the world, who kept up on marketing, social media, human resources, client relations. Meanwhile, a manager would keep things running smoothly, supervising employees, and making sure what was needed for services was operational. Would he retain Esme as that manager? He supposed it depended if the still-to-be-hired director wanted her. His lips pursed at the idea of never seeing Esme again. Although he had no idea why.

What was Jackson planning? Esme wondered. He surveyed the spa as if he was a potential client inquiring about services, not the owner. Perhaps his online files kept him as informed as he needed to be. After all, he seemed disdainful of everything from cucumber water to enzyme scrubs. Was he on the premises to merely refamiliarize himself with the property and layout for the purpose of shutting the spa down? Would he repurpose the space entirely, into offices, shops, even residences if he had the required zoning? Although someone would have to be bonkers anyway to want to alter this gorgeous monument to the city's architectural history.

His personal questions continued. "What got you started in the industry in the first place?"

That shouldn't have been a loaded question but, in her case, it was. "I like spas, where people get taken care of."

"All right, so you could have become, let's say, a doctor or a nurse."

"True, but…" Did she really want to get candid with someone she barely knew and was unlikely to see much of? Still, she had nothing to hide. "I'm not from a family of means. Something like medical school would have been out of our reach."

"Yes, but there are scholarships and loans."

Why was he cross-examining her? "Is that how *you* went to college?"

"I'm very fortunate that my parents sent me to business school to manage our company someday, of course not knowing how soon someday was going to be." She remembered that both of his parents died, his mother not long after Esme had been working for them a year, and his father soon after that. There had been a lot of obvious strife in the Finn family and they had a black cloud over them, from what little she knew.

"Business. Was that your choice of study?"

"It made sense for our family as I'm an only child. The only one who could take over the company."

"Was that what you would have picked if you'd had a choice?" He glared at her, not actually at her, but into her, those luminous dark eyes suddenly fierce as a warrior.

After the awkward silence that followed, where Esme's fingers rolled on little bits of her sweater and he seemed to watch her do so, she realized she was nervous around this forbidding yet troubled man who held her fate. She'd offended him with her too probing question. She wasn't used to interacting with the boss man.

He broke the moment with defense. "Weren't we talking about *you*?"

"The truth is that there was dysfunction in my family and planning for my future was the last thing on my parents' minds." No, Gia and Matt were far too concerned with themselves to have ever put thought into their only daughter's future. "They'd have as soon had me never leave home, so that I could take care of them."

Jackson's expression flickered at her frank answer. "Oh." It was a lot to tell a total stranger. But she learned long ago that the more she threw past trauma out into the ether, into the universe, the less power it held over her.

An elderly woman emerged from the ladies' locker room frazzled and rifling through her purse. Esme rushed over to pick up a few things that had fallen out. "Sit down, Mrs. Lee. You're not at peace. Was something wrong with your treatment today?" She brought the woman to a couch.

"I lost my phone," Mrs. Lee lamented as they sat. "I can never find the darn thing."

"Let's do some breathing and then we'll figure out the phone. With me now, a deep breath in through your nose." She demonstrated and Mrs. Lee followed. "Then a slow exhale through your mouth. Do it again, in through the nose, out through the mouth. Two more times." She glanced up to see Jackson noting the interaction.

"That's better."

"Okay, now, when was the last time you saw the phone?"

"In the locker room. I was calling my daughter to tell her I was finished here."

"Should we have another check in your purse?" Within seconds, Esme located the phone. "There we go."

"Thank you, Esme." She helped Mrs. Lee to her feet.

"See you next time." As she walked the tiny woman toward the exit, Jackson dashed over to the door to open it for her. Hmm. To add to the enigma that was Jackson Finn, apparently, he was a gentleman as well. In the process, his arm brushed against Esme's, creating a shocking prickle down her arm.

"You were saying," he quickly returned after the woman left, "how you got into the industry." He peered down at his arm where it had touched hers as if he was expecting to find something there. The contact had affected him as well.

After she verified that there was, in fact, nothing on his arm other than her aura she answered, "There was a small spa near where I grew up. I got a part-time job there in high school. I mostly did laundry. You'd be amazed at how many towels a spa goes through in a day. I saw people come in color-less and hunched over, and walk out changed, standing tall, smiles rediscovered, as if their burdens had been lifted, even if only tempo-rarily. And I liked that."

She wouldn't share with him the similarity to what went on at her home. Self-centered people having the attention and intention fo-cused on them. That's what Esme was used to and what came naturally to her. Her father *needed* a pizza from Santini's. Her mother *needed* a hot bath drawn for her. Her parents weren't slave drivers; they were just endlessly helpless. Her father wouldn't have had a clue how to order a pizza or even understand how to walk into a pizzeria and wait for his order to be cooked.

They lived on money inherited from Esme's maternal grandparents, who died before she was born. The payout was dispensed monthly with just enough to meet expenses, so that didn't motivate her parents to go out and get jobs. They spent most of their time watching television. Currently, they did so in the ramshackle house that was left to them in Alabama, all they now had, their move allowing Esme to remain in New York and not have to be responsible for them anymore.

She'd always known that she'd get out from under their cloud of listlessness as soon as she was old enough. Taking care of people was the experience she could bring to the job, something she enjoyed as long as it was by choice. Washing towels, mopping floors and restocking products and tools was a start in a business she seemed born to be a part of. Now, at thirty-two, she'd been at the Sher too long, hoping she'd achieve her ultimate goal of becoming a director so that she could create the spa of her dreams. One that would claim her place in the storied history that dated back to medieval times when people would drink and bathe in mineral-rich waters to promote health and healing.

"The work comes naturally to you," he concluded. For reasons that she couldn't name, she wanted to tell him things she'd never told anyone. She wouldn't, of course, but she had never met anyone she'd ever had the urge to confide in. He'd figured her out right away. For a caretaker, the focus was always outward. What was going on with *her* was of no interest to others. Right? That was her role in the world. Except that Jackson was asking. About her. He was listening.

"I went to school to learn massage. I obtained a license in Western modalities and then later another in Eastern traditions."

"You're comfortable touching people you don't know?"

She chuckled nervously. Okay, so she had a one-second idea about touching *him* further than a handshake or a brush of his sleeve. He sure as heck needed to be touched, what with the rigidity in his body that needed loosening up. He was slim but powerfully built; she could see as much under his clothes. "That sort of goes with the territory, doesn't it? We do skin care and bodywork. It involves a lot of touching. And a contract of trust."

"You do the skin care part, too?"

"Yes, over the years I've gotten certified in everything in order to run a full-service spa. When I take time off from here, I go to conferences and trade shows and industry events. Though massage was where I started and it's what always had my heart."

"Impressive that you've taken it upon yourself to continue learning and growing."

"Have you ever had a massage?" Crazy that was a question for a spa owner but she was curious as he'd already declared that this was just another business to him and that it was the Sher Building that had interested his parents, not the spa.

He shrugged. "Here and there. Honestly, they're a waste of time for me. I don't relax. That's not on my agenda. Although…" He let his voice drift off. She was dying to know what it was he stopped himself from saying but it wasn't her place to ask.

"I hope you don't mind me saying so but I do see a lot of tightness in your neck and shoulders. Would you like to lie down or even sit in a chair and let me do a few acupuncture needles and see if I can help out?" At that his eyes froze. She knew she had immediately goofed; that had not been an acceptable offer. Okay, a big businessman does not need an employee to offer to heal him.

Taking care of people.

"Sorry, of course not. That was silly of me."

"Needles?" Oh, he was a needle scaredy-cat! So were many people until they tried it.

"Yes, acupuncture can be an immediate and powerful way to rebalance."

"Not in a million years."

"It was just a thought. My apologies."

"You're qualified to stick needles into people as well?"

"Yes. Acupuncture has been a respected discipline for over three thousand years."

"I'll take your word for that." He tried to chuckle it off. "I think I've seen enough today." He gestured toward the treatment rooms farther down, where, in his mind, sinister and painful things happened. He was quite a bit taller than her so she craned her neck back a little to study him further. Wow, was he gorgeous! Visible stiffness aside. He had smooth golden skin against that dark hair, and a jaw that seemed to catch light. She could detect the slightest five-o'clock shadow in his beard line, but she knew skin well enough to know that his stubble wouldn't have been coarse. Which had nothing to do with anything—he was just an attractive man who crossed her path.

She didn't do men, anyway. The last thing she needed was yet someone else to have to look after, to be used by, to take her attention off herself. No, thanks. Single spa professional was just fine. Which brought her back to the matter at hand.

"Jackson," she began, finally deciding to bite the bullet, "why are you here? Are you shutting the spa's doors? Have you come to fire me?"

CHAPTER THREE

JACKSON STOOD SLACK-JAWED at Esme's question as to whether he'd come to the spa to close it down, and to let her go. His inner staff knew of his plans but he hadn't specifically announced them widely or to Esme when he arrived. His agenda was quite the opposite. Her two-part question was a bit tricky, though. He didn't yet know whether she'd be remaining on staff. She'd held her lovely green eyes open and had boldly and bravely inquired about her future. She deserved a response. He had none for her. "To tell you the truth, I don't know."

"You don't know whether you're closing the spa or you don't know if you're firing me?" One hand moved to her hip in a stance of waiting for his next reply. Which was kind of sexy, her straightforwardness.

"I'm definitely not closing the spa. I'm re-vamping it. I want to take it back to the days when guests came from all over the world."

"What, you're planning to bring in all new people?"

"We want to attract practitioners who have their own client rosters. Each treatment room should be able to generate a lot more revenue than it is now. As to upper management, we're interviewing candidates."

"I see." There was a tinge of sadness in her voice. "When will you know?" Those eyes hooded a bit.

He intended to make the changes and get the new spa up and running quickly. In fact, he'd have to put it to vote with the investors in just a couple of weeks. That deadline was what finally provoked him. As he lay sleepless in bed in a five-star hotel in Croatia, his brainchild began to take shape. That he had to do it for his parents. And, if he was being honest, that he had to do this for himself. Or the stiff neck and shoulders and the chest pains were going to turn into something worse, as his doctor had just confirmed. While he never felt his parents forgave him for the Livia fiasco, they certainly wouldn't have wanted him to die an early death as they had.

He'd do this reimagining with a staff his HR team picked out. He didn't know about Esme's future. She was right to be concerned about her own employment status. "I'll let you know as soon as I can."

She inhaled such a long, slow breath that he could almost see her nostrils fill with air. Then she exhaled like she was blowing up a balloon. Just as she'd done with that older lady who'd gotten upset that she lost her phone. Was it some kind of spa breathing, perhaps meant to steady herself? He'd never dealt with any hirings or firings at the spa; that was left to HR. But he wasn't heartless and didn't need to know how to run a spa to know that people's livelihood was in large measure his responsibility.

"Great," she said, slicing with sarcasm.

She flustered him, a feeling he wasn't used to. *Just leave*, he told himself. He really had nothing more to say right now. Everything wasn't going to be settled today. Something in him didn't want to go, but logic won out. He moved toward the exit. "We'll talk again soon."

"Great," she snapped again, clearly not

saying words that were on the verge of spilling out.

With that, he went out the door and stepped into the elevator that was conveniently waiting. As the doors closed, his neck seized up. He felt bad leaving Esme with such uncertainty but he'd told her all he knew.

For a moment, he wondered what it was like for a client to leave the spa after a transformative treatment. Did they descend from the fifth floor in a euphoria that carried them into the busy, loud and abrasive New York City streets as if they were floating on a cloud? How long did the high last? He wouldn't know from personal experience because he never took a time out. Dr. Singh's words came back to him.

You need to learn to relax.

Maybe he'd get a massage soon, after all. Not from Esme, of course. That would be inappropriately intimate.

As he reached the street, late afternoon was falling to dusk and bustling Tribeca was shrouded by a gray-white sky. He wasn't as eager to leave the area as he thought he was. Instead of returning to his hotel and the many phone calls he had left to accomplish, he spotted the Italian café a few doors down from the Sher. A coffee and perhaps a snack could fortify him until he ordered dinner brought to his suite. The fall chill in the air was mitigated by the heating lamps that stood between every few tables of the café's patio, which was so inviting he sat down before talking himself out of it. He ordered a cappuccino, and then pulled out his phone to talk to his assistant, Kay, with his first question the most topical. "What sort of applications are we getting for spa director?"

"We've got a spa employment agency helping us evaluate. There was a candidate from a hotel spa in Philadelphia, nothing jazzy. A kinesiologist who worked in sports massage with a minor league baseball team. Okay, but she doesn't have spa experience." Jackson thought about Esme telling him that she was trained in both Western and Eastern massage techniques and had her esthetician's license in skin care.

"Are you finding that these people want to bring in their own support staff, like a manager or lead positions?" Again he thought of Esme's welfare and whether she'd be happy working under a spa director.

"Some do, some don't. We got a message from an entire staff of a spa closing in Brazil and they all want to come together but none of them have New York licenses so it wouldn't be easy. We're vetting everyone who applies."

"All right, keep me posted."

He tapped off of the call and stared into the middle distance as he took a sip of the warm cappuccino that had arrived.

Out of the corner of his eye, he spotted Esme coming through the Sher's ground-floor doors to the street. He couldn't help thinking how pretty her hair was, thick, with those caramel highlights. She was really quite beautiful in an organic way. He could imagine holding hands with her in a meadow of waist-high grass. Or splashing naked together in an ocean cove. Kissing under a waterfall. He could tell she was a woman who could make a man *feel*, something to be avoided at all costs. He'd felt enough for one lifetime already. Esme's attractiveness was of no consequence to him. Although it had been strange, the little jolt between them as they were helping that elderly lady out of the spa. Jackson didn't have much touch of any kind in his life. Yet in that moment he'd wanted more from her.

She stopped to button a violet-hued coat

over her clothes and to wrap a multicolored scarf around her neck. For no logical reason he thought of the skin of her throat being protected by woven warmth, and the idea of that gave him a weird contentment.

He hoped she would head down the street in the opposite direction of the café, as they had concluded their discussion for the day. In fact, things had been left on an awkward and uncertain note. Instead, she turned in his direction and wasn't but three steps closer toward him when their eyes met. She nodded in recognition and as she approached the café's outdoor seating area, he felt both compelled and obligated to shout out, "Esme, join me for coffee?"

"Oh. Hi. Okay." She may have felt she had to say yes to the boss but, in any case, she took a seat and ordered a chai latte.

"Do you live around here?" he asked.

"No." She made small talk with, "How long will you be in New York?"

"For as long as this takes. Not letting the spa go to pieces—"

"Excuse me, Jackson," she quickly interrupted, "the spa is not in pieces. In the four years I've been there you haven't given me any upgrading budget or marketing or advertising. I'm doing the best I can with what I have to work with."

Her spunk fired him with energy. "I'm not arguing that, I assure you. What I consider to be our downhill slide began before you were in our employ. And it's my fault for not having corrected that. You've done fine for us."

Her latte arrived and she took a sip as she contemplated what he'd just said. "I just want to be clear that I refuse to be scapegoated for the spa's failings. If you do fire me, I would like to be assured that Finn Enterprises would give me a good recommendation."

Somehow, he already couldn't picture the Sher without Esme, but she was right; she had to think of her own future.

"Absolutely. HR has nothing but respect for you. We wouldn't be taking it lightly if we let anyone go." Respecting employees was something he took seriously.

"Besides bringing on new staff, what are you planning?"

He wasn't prepared to give a presentation although there was no reason to hide his overall plan. In fact, his PR team had already crafted press releases announcing the relaunch of the venerable old spa. Those would go out as soon as the investor group okayed his plans. "I want to know what's out there, what makes the world's best spas *the* best. What we can bring into a city environment. What we can offer that other spas don't."

All of that made sense to him in theory. There was so much to learn. He thought of his parents, who also knew nothing about spas other than that they wanted to own a piece of New York history. Until Livia, with her sleek hair and wandering eyes came along. A master manipulator who sensed that while Jackson was successful and wealthy, he was in need. The medicine he thought she fed him was love but it turned out she only used him, played him like a game. He'd never let that happen again.

"If I may say so," Esme started, then stopped.

"Go on," he urged, interested in what she had to say.

"I think it would be hard for someone who doesn't know spas to reinvent an already existing one."

"I couldn't agree more."

Her attentive eyes got big again. The way the little wisps of her shaggy hair blew this way or that was kind of like watching leaves rustle in the wind, both soothing and majestic. He'd never met anyone who gave off the same essence as she did. Especially while she was facing the possible loss of her job.

"What I'd suggest," Esme told Jackson as they continued sipping their warm drinks, "is that you physically go see some of the world's finest spas. There's only so much you can glean from photos and menus."

He nodded in acknowledgment. After he'd asked her for any suggestions she might have, she was emboldened to share some. Suggestions, ideas, theories, plans, she had plenty of. What she hadn't had was the chance to implement them. She never thought she would at the Sher—her *babysitting* job was clear from the start. Yet she stayed for four years, having got a bit stuck in the sameness. Now the tide was turning whether she was ready for it or not. "I can help provide you with a list if you'd like. I mean, it's all subjective but there are definitely some obvious choices around the globe."

"The trouble is I only have three weeks until I have to take the whole prospect to my investors and get their approval."

"I guess you'd better leave soon, then." She tipped her mouth in a little grin.

Interesting what almost losing their job could do to a person. Instead of being intimidated by the powerful CEO she worked for, she figured she had nothing to lose by showing him how knowledgeable and experienced she actually was. He'd already said that no staffing decisions had been made. It couldn't hurt to dazzle him with her grasp of the industry. Besides, she knew with her contacts and work history, she could find another job. But she didn't want just another job. She wanted to step up. To move forward.

As night fell on Tribeca and they talked and talked, the sky changed from dusk to the indigo of night. Hot drinks at the café turned into two glasses of the house red. Which led to a cheese board, several varieties served on an attractive wooden plank with walnuts on one side and dried apricots on the other, olives and small slices of crusty bread. Once they'd polished that off, Jackson flagged the waiter to order a tiramisu with two forks.

She told him about special spas she knew, about everything from decor to equipment to marketing incentives. It was obvious he didn't know what extractions or fascia stretching were, but he did understand when she talked about promotions and loyalty programs.

"I certainly appreciate your thoughts. How is it that you know all the spas?"

In a flash, she wondered if he'd consider... *No, he probably wanted a fresh start... Although she knew she could...*

The conversation, explaining her world to Jackson, jazzed her up. The change at the Sher was a call to action for her. She couldn't stay in the same place anymore, with all new people above and below her, even if Jackson asked her to. It was time for a revamp of her own. As hard as it might be sometimes, like trying to walk through the molasses of her life, she had to take steps ahead now. The universe was shaking her up. It was time. This was good.

What if...? Could she be that bold...?

As to why she knew the best facilities, the answer was simple. "With my previous jobs and apprenticeships I was able to tour around. It's really a wonderful industry, great people who want each other to succeed. Everybody teaches each other."

"If only my ex-wife thought that way."

"There was a problem, which was why I was hired, right?"

"*Problem* would be an understatement," he let out with a bitter snort of a laugh. "She stole and falsified the books. Good heavens, do all of the staff know about that?"

"Nothing specific. I think everyone knew that the director had been fired for misconduct. Did people know you were married and then, subsequently, divorced?"

"Not many. She'd misled me into believing that she knew something about spas, having estranged parents who were hotel owners. Turns out she knew nothing but since I didn't, either, I was pretty easy to fool. I trusted her. Something I deeply regret."

Ah, so that's why the redo. He felt guilty for both believing his ex-wife was honest and for letting his parents' property devaluate. "Uh-huh," she uttered to encourage him to continue. It was interesting, though, to get the real story.

Esme even observed that between sips of the chianti and a lively volley of chat with her, Jackson's square shoulders settled down and were no longer grazing his ears. She studied that sort of thing in people. It's what made her good at her job. Checking in to what the other person was thinking, doing or feeling. Anticipating.

She had zero interest in men for fear that she'd end up with someone else to take care of, to put first, just as it had been since she was a child. Nonetheless, Jackson had awfully nice shoulders and it gave Esme satisfaction to see them release from their tight hold.

"I was preoccupied with other businesses of ours. I maintained total ignorance of the day-to-day running of the spa. But it gets worse."

"Sorry?"

She watched a series of reactions take over his face. First that jaw cut so exquisitely it could slice ice twitched several times on the right side. Then several blinks of his eyes seemed to further darken his pupils, really actually deaden them. And finally, he settled into a huff of stilted breath wherein she knew he was not going to tell her what *gets worse* about his ex-wife. Although, she was too curious not to try a prompt to get him to continue. "Is that why you don't partake in spa services?"

"I don't have time for spas. Finns work, that's all we do."

"Perhaps *relax* isn't a word that resonates with you. Self-care is essential."

"You sound like my doctor."

"Have you really acknowledged the emotional pain your divorce must have caused?"

"Acknowledged my emotional pain," he repeated as he swirled the last of the tiramisu around the plate with a fork, not wanting to leave anything behind. She liked that he enjoyed his dessert enough to finish it. Even though his tone in repeating her words was a little mocking.

"Have you?" she asked again point-blank. Heck, she was possibly about to be fired or quit; there was no reason to hold back. Something in her had an inkling that if she was able to help him see how restorative, how actually life-changing, a spa could be it might end up being both a good deed and a favorable reflection on her.

"Am I over my divorce? Is that what you're asking?"

"In a nutshell. We carry pain in our minds, in our bodies and in our souls. I'd imagine the body retains energy data for a long time after trauma such as divorce."

"Energy data?"

"Yes. Trauma."

"Trauma. Like the battlefield of war or a child's neglect?"

"Yes. Exactly." A child's neglect. Like her, maybe. Oh, yes, she'd consider herself traumatized.

"So you're likening a divorce from a dishonest woman to being in the middle of, say, a bombing?"

She sat back and folded her arms across her chest. Was this going to be his strategy, to challenge and, in fact, denigrate the work that meant everything to her? "I hear you, Jackson. You don't want to take what I'm saying seriously so you're making fun of it. Yes, people experience trauma from many different causes. It's okay to hang on to it if it feeds you in some way."

"I am not traumatized! I'm just divorced." His eyes shot into hers and she knew that while he was trying to shoo away her words, they had actually penetrated. He ran the back of his hand across his cheek in a motion with a certain tenderness that made her want to reach across the table and do it for him. In reality, he was just buying himself a moment to think. Then, he'd abruptly had enough and returned to an earlier topic, back to business.

"I had intended to hire a spa consultant to help me redesign our style and our menu."

She could play, too. "And your retail, which could be a big moneymaker for you, bring people into the spa, and keep them returning. Right now it's doing none of that. The retail shelves are paltry and ordinary, no products a guest couldn't get somewhere else."

"Okay, menu, look, retail, marketing, all of it."

"And I'd say again, you've gone as far as wanting to make all of those big changes, wouldn't you want to go see for yourself what's out there to compare to?"

"Where would you propose I go?"

"Let me think that all through. For certain, one stop would be Bangkok. Warm rain, juicy fruit, fragrant flowers."

"I take it that's a place you like?"

"What's not to like about Thailand?"

"I've seen the views from the thirtieth floor of a hotel."

She nodded. "I defy you not to enjoy an experience at Spa Malee." At this point she could only ponder his seeming refusal to have any fun at all. No wonder he was tense. She contemplated for a moment if his version of his divorce might be very different than that of his ex-wife's. Maybe she needed what he wasn't able to offer. He did mention she embezzled from him, though. There was no way that could come forth from a marriage of compassion and partnership. "What do you say?"

"I'll consider it." A smile spread across his lips as he removed his napkin from his lap and tossed in onto the table in obvious preparation for leaving. She hadn't seen a spontaneous grin from him. Whoa, when he wasn't trying not to, his smile could light up New York.

They stood and bundled back into their coats. She said a quick goodnight, mentally replaying that smile, as she turned away from him and left.

She called Trevor, her assistant manager, on the subway uptown to where she lived in Washington Heights. "If he invited you to dinner, he must like you."

"He definitely doesn't like me. In fact, I think I made him mad."

"How so?"

"Because I pressed him about whether or not he'd come to fire us."

"Please don't scare me. I have two kids."

He and his husband, Omari, had just adopted twin babies. She had him to worry about, too.

"I don't know what he's thinking at this point. Let's don't borrow trouble yet."

CHAPTER FOUR

"I CAN'T THINK of a reason not to, can you?" Kay responded to the idea that Jackson just threw at her as they held their daily telephone meeting. An idea that Jackson knew was a little funky because he'd felt a sort of woggle in his stomach—or maybe it was lower on his body—when he'd thought of it last night, and the woggle returned as it crossed his mind several times already today. He wasn't sure that was a reason not to go forward, though. Or maybe it was. His brain was a little bit jumbled after yesterday's moonlight over Tribeca.

He'd spent such an unforeseen and interesting evening with Esme, his employee that he barely knew. He'd really never met anyone like her, someone who'd had so many obstacles to overcome and managed to make it through with a level head. Not to mention the fact that his brain had also lingered all day on thoughts of those almond-shaped green eyes that the golden highlights in her brown hair set off. And about the long, delicate fingers that picked at cheese and olives as they chatted.

"Do we have someone who can run things in her absence?"

"There's the assistant manager, Trevor Ames."

"I would just fly around the world with her for a couple of weeks?"

"If that's what you've decided to do. Like you said, go see some spas."

Jackson's wheels were turning. During dinner last night, Esme had mentioned Thailand, and also spa destinations in Sweden and Mexico that she believed were noteworthy. The thoughts of which made him feel a young man's rush about travel and adventure. Totally unlike him, the weary world trekker, lately burnt out on airports and hotels.

Kay intuited that something was going on. "So do you want me to make trip plans?"

"I haven't asked her yet if she wants to go with me." He sounded like a schoolboy inviting a girl to a dance, which made him giddy inside.

He arrived at the spa just before closing time again, not sure why he didn't just text or call Esme. He wanted to ask her in person. Or maybe it was that he wanted to see her today. In any case, she was surprised when he came through the lobby doors. "Oh, hi, Jackson. I wasn't expecting you."

"I have a proposition I wanted to talk to you about."

"I see. Are you firing me?" She said it with that cute lopsided smile so he thought, hoped, that she was kidding and knew today wouldn't be the day of her demise. Hadn't they already established that he didn't know yet whether her job was secure? A client came out from one of the treatment rooms, a woman in black yoga clothes. Esme turned her attention to her. "How was everything, Gwen?"

"Fine. Namaste."

"Namaste." He knew that was a yoga word. After the woman left, Esme turned back around to Jackson. "A proposition." That word sounded loaded coming out of her mouth.

"Can I buy you dinner again, or a glass of wine and we can talk about it?" If she said yes, they could sit down and have a leisurely discussion and lock down the itinerary.

"I'm sorry, I can't. I have plans."

Tightness clenched his gut. He hadn't even told Esme about Livia's betrayal of their marriage vows in addition to the money books. He met a woman he'd naively dared to have faith in. After two years of marriage an old friend informed Jackson that he'd seen her in a booth at a tony restaurant on the Upper East Side passionately kissing a flashy man. When Jackson confronted her about it, she didn't even try to deny it.

The whole thing set off a sickness in him, an acrid dry smell of jealousy and distrust. It kept him from getting close to people. It made him suspicious and skeptical. Irrationally childish, as a matter of fact.

His gut pulsed again. After Livia, he went back to his old self, the businessman who didn't let emotions direct his life. His parents had a marriage devoid of any romance or passion. Devoid of conflict as well, but it was a home run like factory machinery, the wheels on track and on automatic. Livia was a rebellion against all of that. Jackson thought he needed the fireworks that his parents did not. He got way more than he bargained for.

In any case, he needed to not let his silly disappointment show because Esme had evening plans. She was a coworker, nothing more. Although they'd talked last night about personal things, further than Jackson was used to.

"I wanted to get your feedback on something I'm thinking about. Can we at least sit for a few minutes?" He didn't want to schedule an appointment with her for tomorrow. Partially because he was excited about his idea and wanted to share it with her.

"Oh, so you *have* decided you'll fire me?" she asked in a slightly mocking way.

"Stop that." He grinned, again more open than usual. "I already told you it's too early to determine that."

Her smile matched his. He felt a connection in the merge. Like the smiles were reaching each other, like they were meant to. This woman was affecting him in a powerful way so he'd better keep his armor on. She threw him off balance, like the earth under his feet was shifting. The worst part about it was that he liked it.

"What, then?"

"Let's sit down." He gestured to the reception area couches.

"Oh, wow," was the first thing she said after he explained his plan for her to accompany him on the trip and show him the *what* and *why* of her favorite spas. Without too much more deliberation she jumped in with, "Thank you for the vote of confidence and the lovely offer. However, I'll have to say no."

Jackson's jaw slackened. A wave of defeat swept over him. Why had he been so cocky as to assume she would say yes?

She pulled the beige flowy sweater she'd been wrapped in even closer around her. When she focused on responding to him, she talked directly to him, making eye contact. There was something almost unbearable about that directness, nowhere to hide from it. "It's pretty simple. If we were to revisit spas where I've had the good fortune to know the owners and the operators, and they agreed to let you go behind the scenes if you will, that would be a lot to ask. Spa people are incredibly generous, but I can't abuse their comradery."

"I don't exactly follow."

She leaned back on the sofa and tucked her

feet under her legs, like she was settling in to tell him a bedtime story.

"I have to look out for myself. Let's say I cash in on my contacts and they help you build out your menu. And let's say you hire a spa director for the Sher who lets me, and Trevor for that matter, go or I decide to leave. I may need to ask my contacts to help us find work, and to share their own connections with me. I'm going to have to hoard those favors for myself."

Jackson had to admire her foresight. He could see her as a scrappy teenager folding endless carts of towels or refilling massage oil dispensers. How she worked herself up through the ranks to a managerial job in Manhattan.

To the task at hand, though. It would be so valuable to have an industry veteran show him the possibilities. Not to mention the fact that something inside of him was telling him to spend more time with Esme. That she was good for him. Maybe it was his doctor's orders that he learn to replenish his well. Being in the same company as someone who brought that to people for a living could rub off on him. Also, there was something mesmerizing about her. He wanted to know her more. That last bit had nothing to do with the Sher but he acknowledged it, just part of the list of why he didn't seem to want to take no for an answer.

"Esme, there's no circumstance where you could do this with me? I can pay you a huge consulting fee."

"No. Thank you, but that still wouldn't solve my reluctance to overstretch my relationships with people I know in the industry."

They were at an impasse, both playing over things in their minds. "Hmm."

"Hmm."

"Hmm."

"Hmm," she repeated although hers seemed to sound like something was brewing. Then she relented, "Nah."

"What?"

"I do have one scenario in which I'd agree to this."

"What is it?"

"I know it wasn't at all what you were thinking."

"Let's hear it."

"My career goal is to become a director."

"Yes."

"I've been a manager for four years gaining skills and experience. I'm ready for it."

"I don't follow you."

"I'm ready to become a director now." She looked down, then lifted her eyes to meet his again, as if she'd had to summon the courage.

"Uh-huh."

"Are you ready to take a chance on me?"

"What do you mean?"

"If I take you on this trip and we redesign the menu, the style, the way we run the spa, you appoint me as the director and Trevor as manager. You call off your search."

He admired her bravery. "Without interviewing anyone else?" HR had mentioned some other candidates. Shouldn't he at least talk to them?

"I'm qualified. All I need is…opportunity." He wasn't sure why she hesitated for a moment. Maybe her bravado hadn't had a chance to display this much persuasiveness.

"You become the spa director?" He considered it. "I'd have to talk it over with my HR staff."

"You're the boss." That he was. If they'd been sitting in a corner office on the fifty-fifth floor of an office building and she'd just made that pitch to him, he'd hire her on the spot. In his estimation, people who wanted something badly enough did a great job of it.

He got the impression she'd make a very fine director. "What do you think?" she asked him patiently.

Esme let herself into her apartment, still lightheaded from replaying the conversation she'd had with Jackson. Even though she'd met her friend Yina for the movie date they'd planned, her mind hadn't stayed on the screen. She'd wasted ticket money on a movie that may have been very good, may have been very bad and may have been just okay. She wouldn't know.

Plopping down on the sofa, she still couldn't believe that she had point-blank given Jackson Finn an ultimatum. That she'd take him on an odyssey to better understand the spa business and in exchange, if and only if, he'd name her director of the new operation. After all, if she advised him on what was feasible and desired by loyal clients, that would be within the purview of a director's duties, for which she was well ready.

She'd been lolling at the Sher. She well knew what a director did and could have been applying for that position at other spas after her first year or so at the Sher. She'd risen all the way up from washing towels, yet she'd stopped growing. Maybe she was just tired after so many years of hard work and keeping on a happy face, her adult personality miraculously mostly positive. Or perhaps she needed a boost of confidence beyond satisfied clients and cordial industry relationships. Beyond therapy sessions and self-care, the childhood slashes still hurt, crippled her. But now opportunity was roping her along. She was not going to let this pass by, which was why she'd surprised not only Jackson but herself with her steely determination. She had to at least try.

Jackson hadn't answered yes but he hadn't said no, either. She thought she did pretty well at pretending to be courageous when she proposed it to him even though her heart was beating so fast she could hear it in her ears. Of course, he left it hanging and didn't answer right away. That was fair enough. He needed to mull it over.

For now, she looked over to the clock and decided to give herself fifteen minutes of pretending that he'd say yes, letting herself truly experience manifest destiny. Even if it was a fantasy, seeing herself in the role would create something like a memory, making it that much closer to real. She set the timer on her phone and closed her eyes. She saw it, herself welcoming clients to a spa that felt like hers, that she had a stake in, within the walls and under the floorboards.

Lying in bed later, she turned her thoughts from the decision she couldn't control to Jackson himself. His six feet plus of man was warm, strong and inviting with a smell of good soap. Making her feel something inside. Jackson Finn was intense. He made her think about things she'd forbade herself. Denied for her own survival. Even if she was lucky enough to have convinced him to let her have the position and she set off for travel with him, she needed to remember to protect herself first, as surely no one else ever had or ever would. Which meant no personal feelings for a man. That could suck her energy dry.

She and Jackson hadn't made any further plans to meet or talk but she figured the ball was now in his court, as the saying went. Therefore, it was both a surprise and it wasn't when he came through the lobby doors at closing time, as he had for the past two days. His navy blue shirt against his black suit was sexy and stylish.

"Ms. Russo, you drive a hard bargain."

"What?" She didn't want to assume she heard what she thought she heard.

"You drive a hard bargain, but okay. You show me how you'd make this place something spectacular again and I'll give you the reins to it."

A nervous giggle emitted from her that she wished she'd been cool enough to hide. Instead, her stomach flipped over and then back again, and she was sure her face turned beet red. Luckily, she was able to stop from overdoing words and became überprofessional with, "Thank you. You won't regret your decision."

"I hope not. When can you arrange the trip and be ready to leave?"

Whoa, there was so much to do to make that happen. She had to see if Trevor could fill in and make sure her current duties would be covered. She had to make the arrangements with the spas she'd take him to. But she didn't want Jackson to have any reason to hesitate or change his mind so she quickly blurted, "How about the day after tomorrow?" Somehow, she'd pull it together.

"Good." He stayed to walk out with her, watching her go through the tasks of closing for the night. She turned off equipment, locked doors, set alarms and timers on the way out. As they exited, she fumbled to put on her coat. He reached a long arm to pick up the section of sleeve that was dragging and held it open so she could slip one arm in and then the other with ease. Something about the whole maneuver touched deep into her core. He'd noticed that she was having trouble with her coat. He took action to make sure she didn't go out in the cold without it. Someone caring for her. That was a new one.

First order of business was to impress, dazzle in fact, Jackson with her spa tour. She'd already thought of what she'd consider three representations of how unique and special a spa could be. Places that lingered in people's minds for decades, for a lifetime even. That made them dream of returning again and again, and of telling their friends and family about it. Jackson didn't know what would make a spa like that. She'd show him. After meeting spa professionals she'd been invited to visit, shadow and apprentice, she knew a lot of people. On top of that she kept up to date on spa news and had seen photos and menus for hundreds of establishments. Spa was her meat.

"I can tell you right away that we'll be visiting my friend Freja Olsson, who owns Spa Henrik in Stockholm."

"Right, Swedish massage. Even I've heard of that."

"Which wasn't even developed in Sweden but, yes, that will be our starting point for Western-style bodywork."

"Okay."

The last time she'd seen Freja was at a trade show in Las Vegas. Henrik was definitely a world's top pick. Freja was always very generous in giving back to the industry, so Esme was sure she'd be receptive. When she got home it was time to get cracking. It was the middle of the night in Stockholm so she'd fired off a quick text to Freja saying that she'd call her tomorrow but asking if she would be able to spend some time with her and her spa owner, Jackson. Demonstrations of traditional massage would be a good place to start with him.

Esme's mind spun with details as she lugged her favorite suitcase out of the back of her closet. She began unzipping the compartments when her phone rang. The number was not from her contact list. "Hello."

"It's Jackson." Hmm, she had assumed

that their planning had been completed for the day.

"Oh, hi." He hadn't changed his mind about their agreement, had he? That would be devastating. "Can I…help you with something?"

"I was just calling to confirm that I'll have my assistant arrange the flights and book a car to pick you up and take you to the airport." His voice was lower over the phone or perhaps it was just evening. In any case, it was kind of sultry to talk to him over the phone. Seductive.

"Okay."

"You'll arrange everything with the spas?" Again, his voice was so resonant it was blowing through the phone like warm air, filling not only her suitcase but her entire bedroom. In fact, his tone prompted her to take off the sweater she still had on. She doubted he knew how magnetic he was. His charisma was something she needed to watch out for. She was not going to have a crush on the boss. There was too much at stake.

"Yes, I've already left a message for Freja in Stockholm."

"Send me all the travel bills, of course."

"So does your company have, like, a private plane?" She didn't really know much about Finn Enterprises on the whole.

"No, we're not at that level." His response came with a laugh that was friendly not scolding. "I can promise you the first-class cabin on all the flights, though."

"And I can promise you the best spa services you're ever likely to encounter."

"Wait. I have to receive the treatments myself?"

She smiled to herself. "Well, of course, Jackson. I want you to experience for yourself how good and beneficial these protocols are."

"How about we do them on you and you can sort of narrate for me?"

"No siree," she teased, remembering how resistant he was to let her do acupuncture or even massage on his tense shoulders. And what shoulders they were. She pictured his long, lean body. She wondered if he was calling her from an office or a hotel room. Was he at a desk, or a sofa or…in bed? What was he wearing? She mashed her lips for a minute, hardly believing she was having those thoughts. So unlike her. She forged on with, "Will you have the treatments I choose for you? That's the whole point. Besides, your doctor would approve, wouldn't he?"

She could practically see his thousand-watt smile take over. "Oh, all right. What should I pack?"

That was a valid question as his fine suits and smudgeless dress shoes didn't scream relaxation. "Do you have casual clothes?"

"What kind of question is that?"

"You've said you're all work and no play."

"True, but I do business all over the world with all sorts of people. Of course I have casual clothes."

"Great. Let's put them to proper use, then." And in quick succession she pictured him in a ski outfit. In loose-fitting yoga pants. In just a towel slung low across his hips. Wicked musings that had no place in her dealings with him. Her tongue made a once-around her lips. She resuscitated herself with, "Stockholm in autumn will be colder than New York so you'll need outerwear, but Mexico and Thailand will be warmer."

"All right, I'll check in with you tomorrow."

"Good night, Jackson."

As she swiped off the phone she thought this could all go well or it could go horribly if Jackson wasn't impressed with the trip. It was a crossroads for her. A person didn't get many of those in their life. A way to turn the corner and cumulate the past into something that served the future. It was possible that Esme Russo had officially, finally, arrived.

CHAPTER FIVE

"GOOD MORNING." Esme greeted Jackson at the airport lounge before the flight as agreed. "Everything good?"

They hadn't talked yesterday after that flirty phone call the night before, just sent a couple of texts.

"Yes."

He gestured for her to accompany him down the jet bridge, onto the plane and into the first-class cabin, him flashing the boarding passes on his phone. He watched her take stock of their surroundings. The appointments were deluxe on this aircraft bound for Stockholm. A table between the two seats was set with a bottle of champagne and two flutes. It was almost, well…romantic. He was suddenly unsure about this strange journey that forty-eight hours ago he would have never imagined himself taking.

Not to mention the promise he'd made to her about the directorship. No sooner had he instructed his HR people to launch a search for the right person than he'd told them to halt the hunt, at least for now. It occurred to him, though, that had Finn Enterprises announced that they were hiring a spa director, perhaps Esme would have formally applied for the position anyway. He may have been saving time even if he'd acted uncharacteristically impulsive in saying yes to her. They'd both better be right as there was no time to lose before the investors meeting.

Once they were in the air, he tipped open his laptop and logged into the plane's Wi-Fi as soon as it was available. He'd work, slip into his cocoon for a while. Hours passed. He noticed Esme watch a movie from start to finish and then do something on her tablet. They chatted briefly about the food and drink they were served and that they'd both been to Stockholm before. However, neither knew the city well and there wouldn't be time for much exploring. At one point, the flight crew passed out hot facecloths, which he disregarded.

"This is always a nice touch," Esme commented. "Flying can be dehydrating to the skin."

"Good to know," he said, glancing over at her. Which there was no denying was a very pleasant activity.

Observing that he didn't pick up his hot towel she asked, "Why aren't you using yours?"

"I wasn't aware my skin was being dehydrated so it wasn't a crisis that needed resolving."

"Very funny. Remember, you're to pay more attention to your wellness."

"I do. It's a policy of distrust and jealousy that I rely on." Wow, that was sharp. Even she seemed taken aback. Who had he become, just a sarcastic and bitter shell with health problems? That was no way to live. Especially not at thirty-three. Esme's basic humanity and lack of pretension made him want to tell her more of what he had stashed inside. She'd told him on the phone that he'd be actually receiving the spa ministrations she thought so highly of. He didn't even know what had propelled him to call her at home. They'd laughed a bit about his aversion to therapies. Talking to her came easy to him. He picked up the hot, wet washcloth and brought it to his face. He wiped in big circles, a few times. He had to admit that it was pleasant. Not necessarily healing, as Esme would say, but nice nonetheless.

"See, not half-bad," she ribbed him sweetly. Her little told-you-so smile was adorable and sent a pang through him. "Distrust and jealousy, huh? Is that a blanket statement? Does that mean you don't trust me? Don't you think that if I was going to steal from you that after four years I would have done it already?"

"Fine. I didn't mean trusted employees, although—" he wasn't ready to share that one with her "—suffice it to say I'll never be in a personal relationship again. It clouds my judgment."

"I'll give you that—neither will I. But actively married to distrust and jealousy, do you know how toxic that is?"

"Toxic."

"Those kinds of emotions fire off your adrenal glands, which weakens your immune system and makes you especially vulnerable to autoimmune disease."

"And it's your position that you can just let go of that with a wet washcloth?"

"No, but finding techniques that give you

a respite from all of that really does make a difference. There are thousands of studies on it. You've been working nonstop since take-off. How about stretching your arms above your head?" She demonstrated and he followed. "Let go, and then arch your back. Rotate your neck. Little changes add up."

"I didn't tell you all about my failed marriage." The words were on the tip of his tongue until they just fell out. Was it the hot towel or the stretching that opened him up a little, like his lungs could take in more air? Or was it her, pulling him along? "Not only did Livia betray me with the spa finances, she didn't honor our marriage vows."

"What do you mean?"

"Forsaking all others. She didn't."

"You mean she cheated on you?"

"All over town." No wonder he'd avoided New York until now.

"Oh, Jackson, that's awful. Was it just once?"

"No, it went on for months until I learned of it." He had no idea what a relief it would be to say all of that out loud to someone. Not anyone, of course. Her.

"How did you find out?"

"A friend spotted her kissing someone at a restaurant."

"In plain sight?" She put her hand over her mouth, taking it all in.

"No regard for the decency of marriage."

"Then what happened?"

"Livia didn't even try to deny it. Although she didn't admit to the spa's bookkeeping irregularities that were uncovered at that time. Because she knew that she and whatever man she'd taken up with, her partner in crime, had committed illegal acts. We could have had her arrested but we didn't want to draw attention to ourselves, which we knew the whole mess would."

"Jackson, how awful." She looked at him with concern, or maybe it was pity. "Then what?"

"Very simple at that point. I had her out of the spa, changed the locking codes, took her off the bank accounts and so on." In his gut he wanted to keep talking to Esme even though he was embarrassed that he'd picked such a crooked person to marry. Esme had that way about her, like she was receptive and she could handle someone else's pain. She'd mentioned the neediness of her own parents shaping her into that caretaker she'd become and that she had parlayed it into a spa career. He hoped, in turn, she had people she could tell her secrets and hurts to. For reasons that made no sense he wondered if he could ever be that person for someone.

Not someone.

Her.

"You're having emotions about it now." Was she looking into his third eye or something?

"Frankly, the whole thing left me with my guard up, which is how I plan to stay." A way he thought was serving to protect him. In a moment of clarity, he realized how instead it was holding him in shackles. "I surely won't make the same mistake twice."

"At the expense of your health and well-being?" He was suddenly aware of her close proximity. He could almost feel her body heat. He'd bet her skin and her hair were as silky as they looked.

"What about *your* internal trauma?" he repeated, employing terminology that she'd used.

"You want to know something?" He surely did, ready to take the focus off himself. "I know all about jealousy. That was a little trick my parents used to play on each other.

Fight for my attention and loyalty to make the other one jealous. I don't know what's worse, romantic jealousy or pitting your kid against your spouse." The heavy statement weighed like a brick and he ached for her.

Couldn't they both use a little fun on this trip? Doctor's orders, after all. Strictly professional, of course. Maybe he wasn't going to be as resistant to spa life as he thought he was. Or maybe something else was hammering at his walls, trying to tear them down.

"Ladies and gentlemen," came the pilot's voice over the sound system, "we have begun our descent into Stockholm's Arlanda Airport."

"I take it we're in Stockholm because the term *Swedish massage* is best known to people," Jackson asked as they stepped out of the taxi in front of Spa Henrik, their first destination.

"Yes," Esme acknowledged, "although there are some historical questions as to whether that namesake massage was really developed in Sweden or just popularized here. No matter, though, it's accepted as the traditional Western massage." The snowy and cold weather made their breath visible. The clean air of Stockholm was invigorating.

The spa was housed in a Gustavian building, the city's classic architectural style,
and they buzzed the intercom at the spa's
entrance. Once Esme announced them, the
door clicked and they entered a long hall of
rooms with wooden doorframes and wood
floors. She remembered from her visit years
ago when she was doing an apprenticeship
in Copenhagen that the minute she'd stepped
into Spa Henrik, the outside world faded
away. Perhaps it was the hush of the high
ceilings combined with the thickness of the
walls. She and Jackson moved toward the reception lobby. "See how this place just sucks
you in. Makes you forget where you are. I'd
like for us to be able to create that. Envelop
people so they can leave their everyday lives
at the door for a while."

Jackson took in the information. What she
was ready to show him was her vision of a
future for the Sher, something she'd thought
about for a long time. He'd either be impressed enough with what she presented to
him that he'd agree to implement it and let it
rest in her arms or he'd reject everything she
suggested and choose another spa director
with a different perspective. She'd decided
that she wouldn't stay if she wasn't offered

the directorship. Not after four years of being the manager. The humiliation of being passed over would be too difficult. It would be her sign to move on. This was the beginning or the end for her.

It was fitting that she was now walking the hallway of Freja's spa. When she'd come to Europe and taken the same footsteps years ago, straight after getting her first license, she was just learning the hierarchy of the industry. And now there was the possibility that a facility would be placed completely in her hands. To nurture like her offspring. Putting those hard-learned caretaking skills to use, with a spa baby of her own.

When they reached the welcome lobby she said to the receptionist, "*Hej.* Freja is expecting us." The young woman pressed a button.

"Esme!" The familiar voice called out as Freja appeared from an inner office.

"Freja! Gorgeous as ever."

Freja Olsson approached. She was a tall, thin reed of a woman in an outfit of dark leggings and a flowing white blouse with sandals despite the outdoor temperature. She moved swiftly with a kind of hips-forward gait that belied her age. Esme estimated she was in her mid-seventies. They embraced,

Freja pulling her close and pressing Esme into the narrowness of her bony body. "I want you to meet Jackson Finn."

"A pleasure." Jackson put out his hand for a shake but Freja bypassed it completely and embraced him as well. Esme could tell Jackson was tentative and leaned forward for the hug rather than allowing his entire body to make contact with hers. He'd said he didn't have a lot of touch in his life, one reason he didn't like bodywork. He'd even initially pooh-poohed using a hot washcloth on his face during the flight.

But then, goodness, had he opened up, telling her buried secrets he must have been holding for years. He wouldn't recognize it yet but that was probably as valuable to him as the most penetrating massage. Plus, they had some inherent similarities, minus the cheating spouse for her, but finding those was cathartic to her, too, which was not unwelcome. She'd learned not to dredge up her past too often but, on occasion, the fellowship was reassuring.

"The spa was established by my grandfather in 1928. We've resisted modernizing and made as few changes as possible."

"Oh, I don't think that's so," Esme countered. "What about your cutting-edge skin care regimes?"

Esme's heart was in bodywork, but many spa users came through the doors for skin care. It was a huge source of revenue. "Jackson, Freja and I texted yesterday about giving you a massage and her men's facial."

"You'd be demonstrating the treatments on me?" He pretended to be in shock.

"Yes, darling," Freja answered.

"Wait, did we agree to that?" Esme could tell he was only halfheartedly protesting.

"We talked about it on the phone the other night," she reminded him. During that strange phone call when his voice crawled all over her. He shrugged and put his palms up as if in surrender. The three of them chuckled.

"You're in good hands," Esme promised.

"We'll begin with a massage," Freja instructed. "Do you prefer a male or female therapist?"

"Male," he answered at bullet speed. Esme knew that men were often uncomfortable being treated by women and vice versa. No doubt stemming from the seedy and inappropriate shenanigans that sometimes took place in what was incorrectly called a massage parlor. Esme, Freja and everyone they knew, had ever known, were absolute professionals. In her career Esme had never even heard of any improper behavior. Still, the reputation lingered and she'd had occasion to have to assure clients of their safety. In a spa setting, sometimes the client preferred the smaller, softer hands of a woman or the opposite, the strength and size of a man's.

Freja led them to the dressing room. "Use any of the lockers you want. Please take a robe. Generally, we prefer the access of a nude body, at all times covered with a sheet, but you're more than welcome to leave your underwear on if that makes you feel more comfortable."

"Jackson—" Esme wanted to check in as well "—we were planning to meet you at the massage table so we could talk about the session as it happens. To give you a sense of how we work. Is that okay with you?"

He definitely took a moment to digest it all and she couldn't blame him. He'd be naked under a sheet with an unfamiliar man's hands on him and two women watching. Spa people had a very clinical, medical view of it all but she was sensitive to the fact that he might not. Yet, anyway.

He nodded, "When in Rom— Stockholm."

"Anders will be your therapist today," Freja announced as a big strapping blond man entered the room. He wore a blue uniform shirt not unlike a hospital scrub that bore the insignia of Spa Henrik, a pair of hands joined together to resemble a heart. Underneath, he wore black pants.

Esme had never met Anders but she knew that Freja would have brought in one of her top people for this demonstration. "Nice to meet you," Esme said to him with a polite smile. Jackson watched her every move as she interacted with the man. In fact, he scrutinized Anders from head to toe before extending his own hello.

"If you'll lie face down on the massage table." Anders pointed. He helped Jackson lie down on the padded table and removed his robe at the same time as he covered him with sheets, leaving only his head and the bottoms of his feet exposed. "Are you comfortable?"

Jackson fit his face into the cradle of the headrest, a horseshoe shape that allowed the recipient to breathe fresh air while their head, neck and torso remained aligned. "I'm all right."

Anders brought his oils on a trolley next to the table. "Do you have any allergies?"

"No."

"Anders is asking that," Esme explained, "because he'll be using oils to lubricate your skin and facilitate his hands' movements on you. Some people are very sensitive to certain products or scents."

"I use a sweet almond oil as my base," Freja said. "Then I can add other oils for aroma or skin care properties. Almond is not the cheapest, that's for sure, but it's worth it."

Anders pumped oil from a dispenser and rubbed his hands together to warm it. "Let's begin."

"We start with effleurage," Freja began her narration, "which is the technique of using long gliding strokes along the curves of the body aimed toward the heart. This promotes relaxation and allows the therapist to get to know the client's body and where there might be tension. The oil gives us a way to warm the muscles."

Esme chimed in, "Also, we can learn if the client prefers light or firm pressure. A massage that uses heavy pressure is called deep tissue."

Freja continued, "The idea of calming the

muscles manually is part of the Western style of massage, which looks at physiology and understanding of body mechanics. As opposed to the Eastern philosophies, which approach health by analyzing the life force, and flow or blockage of energy." As was proper protocol, Anders worked on a section of Jackson's body at a time, removing and then recovering parts with the sheet and uncovering others. He moved to each arm and leg and then his back to take inventory of Jackson's physique and where he was holding tightness or misalignment. "Next, we'll go to the technique called petrissage. Here we lift and knead the muscles and fascia to draw blood to the area, which promotes all-body release."

"How are you feeling, Jackson?" Esme asked, wanting to check in because he claimed not to see value in massage at all so she hoped this was helping to change his mind.

"It's fine." His voice sounded strained or maybe constricted. Esme hoped he didn't have his mind on work or on his ex-wife and the atrocity he'd told her about. Although he wasn't the easiest person, he certainly seemed honest so it was a shame that he put his faith in the wrong person. Although she understood plenty about not being able to count on people. Her parents took advantage of a child's innate trust.

Eventually, Anders explained the next phase. "We'll move on to tapotement. I'm sure you've experienced this rhythmic tapping. My hands are in what people call karate chop position. I move quickly up and down a large area to awaken the soft tissue after we've increased the blood flow. To create vibration within the body, which is profoundly restorative."

"With massage," Esme said, "we address muscles and tendons and ligaments and joints and connective tissue all at once. And the process reduces constriction to both the body and mind."

It was a lot to take in so after that they stayed quiet while Anders continued until he finished the session.

CHAPTER SIX

"HOW WAS THAT for you?" Freja asked after Jackson's massage demonstration.

Jackson didn't know what to say to these people for whom that question was of the utmost importance. *Fine* was not going to be an acceptable answer. Although, that's what he thought. It was soothing to have his muscles worked on by Anders, obviously a skilled professional who knew exactly what Jackson's body needed. But Jackson didn't feel like he'd had a monumental *aha* about it. That was okay. He found the details very interesting.

What he wished was that he hadn't winced to himself when Anders smiled at Esme for a little too long as they were introduced. He'd had a silly stab of jealousy at that, which was absurd on so many levels. First and foremost, he had no attachment to her other than as coworkers. She was an independent woman responsible for herself. Second, just because Livia had cheated on him didn't mean that every woman he got near was going to hurt or betray or double-cross him. His intellectual mind knew that. His mere acquaintance with Esme shouldn't be unearthing those demons. After all, he had many women in the company's employ. He hadn't exactly figured out what triggered him with Esme. It was a kooky yet instinctive response. Also, Esme had mentioned her parents pitting her against one another to make the other jealous. Which was sick and cruel and something she didn't need any more of in her life. He needed to nip his immature feelings in the bud right here and now.

As Esme had pointed out, he'd trusted her as an employee and that's all that mattered. He could trust her with the spa but not trust her with his heart. This had nothing to do with their personal lives. Which, in turn, had nothing to do with each other. Yet the mere thought of that made him sad.

"Marvelous," he answered Freja's question, not wanting to negate anything that had transpired.

"Would you like to do some inhaling in our salt room?"

Inhaling. Yes, he supposed he'd like to do some inhaling. So as not to die, that was. "What I'd like to do is eat."

"Wonderful. We have our spa café on the lower floor. Let me inform the chef right now that you're on your way down and she'll prepare a sample menu if that's all right." Freja drew her phone from her pocket and punched in.

"Jackson," Esme piped up, "why don't you stay in your robe and have that experience? Often people come to a day spa and spend hours there, keeping it fluid between treatments and their own leisurely pursuits. Many spas have extra features like meditation rooms, steam chambers, whirlpools, saunas and classes. Freja has a juice bar and a full-service restaurant for spa cuisine where it is absolutely acceptable, encouraged even, to eat in your robe and leave your belongings in the locker."

"Does *spa cuisine* mean I will still be hungry afterward?"

She chuckled, which was his intention. "People do tend to eat light and fresh at the spa. You can imagine that a massage might not feel as good on a stomach that was digesting a lot of food."

Freja said, "I promise to fill you with foods that will increase your vitality and be kind to your digestive system."

"Oh, so I'll certainly be hungry afterward," he said forcing his eyes wide open to make Esme giggle again. He couldn't think of the last time he purposely tried to make someone laugh. Maybe that massage had loosened him up some after all.

"Let's go." Freja led them down a flight of stone steps to the lower level, which was hushed with an almost echo. An enormous vase of yellow, gold and white flowers welcomed guests to the restaurant area.

"Beautiful blooms," Esme commented.

Freja pointed to a side door that led to another staircase. "Non-spa clients can enter here from the street. The restaurant provides good cash flow for us because people from the nearby office buildings and shopping districts come to the restaurant for lunch."

"That's not something we'd be able to do," Esme added. "I just wanted to mention what some people are doing to increase profits."

Freja spoke to the chef and then she sat them

at a blond wood table with padded chrome chairs.

"Thank you, Freja," Esme said to her friend. Esme had such warmth about her, it seemed to emanate from every inch of her. He'd never been around someone like that. His parents were as cold as ice. Esme touched his heat inside. He wanted to wrap his arms around her as if he was a giant winged bird and could envelop her in his span. When she asked which was worse, being cheated on or being betrayed as a child, his heart clenched. As she'd said, she turned around the childhood of having to care for some selfish people to a vocation of taking care of others. Was she taking good enough care of herself?

At the Sher a couple of days ago, her eyes misted with tears after he'd helped her put on a coat that she'd been struggling with. Was she so unaccustomed to kindness toward her that even such a small gesture was a big deal? He was just being decent in seeing that she could use a hand. It was hardly a heroic act. While his parents were stoic, they were at least well mannered. And the funny thing was, after he helped her get her coat on he wanted to do more for her. He wanted to lay his own coat down on a puddle in the street so she could step over it. Or give her the imaginary gloves he had on to keep her hands warm.

He looked at her across the table. Yes, he'd like to keep her warm.

Then he blinked his eyes open. What kind of crazy fantasy had he just had? He needed lunch.

A waiter brought two glasses of water in goblets. Jackson downed his in one sip. "Hmm. Room temperature?"

"We can request ice if you'd like. Freja thinks icy drinks are too shocking for the organs."

Next the waiter placed a small plate in front of each of them. "This is our farm-to-table quinoa beet bowl with fresh picked kale." As he'd feared, rabbit food. Kale was supposed to be a garnish on the side of the plate! "With an avocado goddess sauce." He had no idea what that meant but he liked avocado and there was definitely something goddess-like about Esme.

"Thank you." He'd give it a try.

The waiter stepped away and returned with two tall narrow glasses of a milky pink drink. "Our antioxidant berry lassi."

Jackson sipped it, a delicious smoothie that

managed to be creamy, tart and sweet all at once. That wasn't as hard to get down as the kale. Wasn't Swedish food heavy and hearty, to combat the cold winter? He'd go get two dozen meatballs later.

Since he was stuck here for the moment, in a robe no less, as Esme gamely chewed her weed salad, he asked, "You and Freja began to explain about the variety of massage techniques. What are some other types besides Swedish?"

"I think we were explaining deep tissue. That's when we'll use more pressure. In doing that, we can better relieve pain or chronic stiffness and concentrate on one area of the body."

The enthusiasm in Esme's voice made him want to keep her talking. He could listen to her for hours. "What else?"

"Well, there's trigger points where we work on one part of the body to assist another. For example, relieving pressure on the neck can help with the frequency and duration of persistent headaches."

He creaked his head to stretch out his neck in one direction and then the other. He had to admit that he felt more range of motion after that massage than he had in a while. "Interesting."

"I can see that your neck bands are more fluid," she said in response to his stretching.

"It amazes me that you can glean that from across the table."

"You have chronic stress, Jackson. I could tell from the minute you walked into the spa. What are you doing to relieve it?"

"I had been doing nothing. Now my doctor is warning me what could happen if I don't address it."

"What will you do?"

"I'm supposed to do relaxing things. Take more vacations. So, hey, this counts as a vacation, doesn't it?"

"Not based on how much time you spent on your computer during the flight."

"Do you have the magical, mystical work-life balance that everyone is so highly touting?"

"I don't know that it's so idyllic for anyone. But I take yoga and I practice mindful breathing."

"What's that?"

"Slowly breathing in through your nose and just as slowly out through your mouth."

"You were doing that with that elderly lady at the Sher."

"Try it with me. In through the nose." They both inhaled. "And out through the mouth." They exhaled.

"Okay."

"And you do it as many times as you need to. It will transport you, I promise." She took a few bites of her food.

He used his fork to isolate a couple of chunks of avocado and brought them to his mouth. "Tell me about other treatments."

"People have been using heat and cold as body therapies for thousands of years. A simple, non-messy and effective way we can deliver that is with hot stones."

"How do you use them?" He looked at his bowl while visualizing a big plate of bacon and eggs. "Are there twigs in this?" He scrunched up his face and got another smirk out of her.

She pressed on. "We place warmed stones on parts of the body where we want to open soft tissue and increase blood flow."

"Are there particular kinds of stones?" He managed another bite of the bunny food, fascinated by listening to Esme. He thought back to that first night with her in New York when a coffee at the Italian place turned into delicious wine and dinner. They'd shared a tiramisu dessert, a rather familiar act for two people who barely knew each other. Yet he'd relished it, hadn't realized how much he craved simple, honest conversation. A face across the table. He was a boss to many but friend to few.

"Really almost any smooth stone is fine but the industry standard is basalt, which is heavy and volcanic."

She was so truly passionate about her work. He loved that she'd found what she wanted to do with her life at an early age and was doing it. And that she was gutsy enough to stand up to him, to tell him that she'd take him on this trip only with the promise that if he liked her ideas, he'd name her spa director afterward.

"That sounds like it would be a unique sensation."

He sensed she was enjoying sharing her expertise with him. "Let's see," she continued. "Any spa session can be enhanced with aromatherapy." Thankfully, the waiter noticed that Jackson wasn't eating the garden in a bowl and brought another berry lassi and a plate of crackers and nuts. "We use scent to awaken the sense of smell along with everything else we're doing. For example, lavender is known to produce calm whereas citrus is a wake-up call."

"What about you, Esme? What's your favorite kind of massage?"

She looked at him as if no one had ever asked her that question. Which brought back his musings that if she was busy caring for other people, who was caring for her? Was she as complete as she fronted she was? He doubted it. Just like him. They were quite a pair.

"Thanks for asking. Actually, it's the Thai style. Bangkok will be our last stop on this trip so I'll have a chance to show you. It's a guided-movement practice performed on the floor with the recipient in loose clothing."

"What do you like about it?"

"To each his own but for me, the manipulation of my movements is so therapeutic."

He felt a surge of excitement, as if he'd never traveled to the ends of the earth which, in fact, he had. Never with her, though. Her spirit was infectious.

"Please," Freja said and gestured, "get comfortable in the facial chair." After lunch, it was time for Jackson's skin care treatment, which Freja was going to perform herself. He sat down and she used the controls to recline him and elevate his legs.

"This is like being at the dentist," Jackson said, "which, by the way, I hate." He snarled at Esme like a grouch. She gave him a thumbs-up signal.

"Some clients prefer to use earbuds and listen to their choice of music or spoken word, guided meditations," Freja said, "while they're having the treatment. Of course today, we want to talk to you about the protocol."

"Yup."

"We'll start with a thorough cleansing," Freja explained as she began. "I've got half a dozen cleansers here and I'll choose which one to use based on the client's skin type. Jackson, I can see that your skin runs a little dry so I'm going to use a product that I know is moisturizing. I'll blend that in all across your face starting with the neck and working my way upward. We want to completely clean the face and beard area. How does that feel?"

"Strange."

As she moved across his face she continued, "Skin has a lot of impurities. I can see that you hold some deep grime, as we do in the cities. I also see patches of dehydration, which can be caused by a lot of travel and also from poor sleep."

"Check and check. You can tell that from my skin?"

"Skin works hard. It can become fatigued. It needs attention." She used wet disposable sponges to remove the cleanser. And followed that with a calming toner applied with cotton balls.

"Now she's going to use a polyhydroxy compound, which won't further dry out sensitive skin," Esme narrated. "What we need to do is exfoliate, meaning slough off the dead skin so that we can bring out the healthy cells underneath."

"Are you painting my face?" Jackson reacted to the small brush Freja was using to apply the product.

"As a matter of fact, I am."

"Would you like to see yourself in a mirror?" She didn't wait and grabbed a handheld mirror from the counter. She handed it to Jackson, who shimmied in disbelief that the so-called gentle exfoliator was…bright yellow, covering his face from forehead to clavicle, except around his eyes and mouth.

"I look like a lemon!"

Esme reached over to lay a reassuring hand on his arm. "What happens in the spa stays in the spa." She had to tell herself to take her hand back. It wanted to stay there.

"Now, we'll do the extractions." Freja pulled her wheeled work trolley over and began to position her lighted magnifying lamp correctly to view his face. "This is often what clients find to be the most uncomfortable part of the facial and so they opt out of it. But there's nothing that replaces removing blackheads and other pollutants one at a time. May I continue?"

"I suppose, although you're scaring me," he answered with trepidation. After covering his eyes with cotton pads so the rays of her lamp didn't bother him, she used the magnifier to locate, and then used her metal extraction tool to scrape off the blackheads and clogged pores she found on his face. "Yikes," he commented immediately on his discomfort.

Esme couldn't disagree. But she wanted Jackson to understand the skin care component to the spa menu. "Very often clients book both facial and bodywork sessions for the same day."

"Are we done yet?" Jackson all but pleaded as Freja picked and picked until she was satisfied.

"Now we'll do a gel mask for hydration. It uses algae to firm, lift and brighten the skin."

"You're putting seaweed on me?"

"It's a nutrient-rich ingredient that yields fabulous results. Another thing I think would benefit your skin is microneedling."

"Does that have the word *needle* in it? I already don't like it." No more than he had liked Esme's suggestion of acupuncture the other day.

She showed him the penlike tool used for that process. "See, it has tiny needles. We brush the skin making minuscule punctures which stimulate the skin to produce collagen to heal them."

"Punctures. I'll take your word for that." He jumped out of the chair.

"Thank you for bearing with us." Esme wanted to hug him but he'd suffered enough, she laughed to herself.

After he showered and dressed, they decided to walk to their hotel despite the cold. They strolled through the Gamla Stan, Stockholm's Old Town, with its cobblestoned alleys and buildings of muted colors and carved wood. The air was filled with brisk flurries of snow.

One minute they were walking forward, continuing to talk about spa operations and then, really not meaning to, he took Esme's hand. Her skin was unspeakably satiny. He shot his eyes over to her for approval. She looked down at their entwined hands, as surprised as he was, like a force in and of itself had made the move, neither of them having anything to do with it. A bit like the energy wave that had passed between them at having brushed against each other at the Sher that first day. The thing was, it felt absolutely natural, normal and right. As if their hands had been searching for each other since the beginning of time. Like they had each been lost and finally found their way home.

A peace came across his face that he could actually feel, another move happening without him consciously instructing it to. He stopped walking, which pulled her a little closer to him. Still holding one hand, he took hold of the other to make their two spheres form a circle. And when his face drew just a few inches from hers, he kissed her. A quick wisp of a kiss, just letting his mouth make contact with the velvet that was her lips. His eyelids fluttered because he liked it so much, the smallness of the action becoming a still photo. His brain told him that the earth had, in fact, shifted. That there would forever be this instant. The timeline in the history of the world would now be divided between having not yet stood on the street in Stockholm in the snow kissing Esme Russo, and then time forever after it occurred.

He kissed her again, let his lips linger a bit longer, to feel the press of their mouths against each other. His tongue flicked a snowflake from her upper lip. One of his hands disentangled from hers in order to cup her cheek, downy, pillowy and cold at the same time. He brought her face closer, this time to kiss deeper, to kiss longer, letting himself swell with the desire to keep kissing her.

As the snowflakes fell, cascading them with powder, they kissed and then kissed some more. Until there was actually no weather, no sky, no Stockholm—there was only their bodies against each other, two as one.

Then, suddenly, after they'd been standing in that one spot for who knows how long, some kind of awareness took over Esme. She pulled her head back, creating an undeniable space between them, a chasm. The moment was over. Definitely and completely over. "Jackson, I don't..." She struggled for words, taking in one of her slow inhales and exhales. "I don't... With men... I don't really...date."

His mouth fell into a circle like a surprised child, shocked by the kissing he'd instigated and even more shocked by her abrupt end to it. "Oh, was dating what we were doing?"

"And then there's lymphatic drainage, reiki, reflexology, shiatsu..." Esme forced herself to stop babbling as she and Jackson continued their walk.

"Uh-huh."

There weren't many people on the street; it was too cold. She knew she'd been talking a mile a minute as snowflakes whooshed around them. She was doing anything to avoid dealing with what had just happened.

He'd kissed her, with a fire that could have melted the snow around them for a five-foot radius. It had been a long time since Esme had been kissed by anyone. And she'd never been kissed like that, with a force and passion that she'd only seen in a movie or read in a book, nothing she'd ever thought was real.

It wasn't true when she told him that she didn't date. New York married friends always knew a great guy they wanted to introduce her to. The trouble was she never connected with any of them, never found any Venn diagram where their worlds overlapped. She wasn't interested in what they cared about and it appeared to be vice versa. Or worse still, they were needy and once her elemental competence was visible, they'd started wanting her to be their mother or at least their social director. In any case, it had been a long time since she'd even exchanged that with a man.

She decided to bite the bullet with Jackson, stop blathering about spas, and get said what needed to be expressed. After all, they were leaving for Mexico in the morning, and had the rest of the trip to get through and then a possible long-term working relationship. They had to get past what had just transpired. "So hey, you asked me if what we just did was dating? What did you mean by that?"

He glanced over to her as they walked, and then returned to facing forward so he didn't have to make eye contact. "I don't know. I just wanted to be clear with you. What just happened…"

"You kissed me," she jumped in. "Out of the blue."

"Did I? I can't remember how it started."

"What do you mean, you can't remember? We were walking and then we were kissing."

"Did I do something improper?"

"I suppose it could have been. I didn't regard it as such."

"So you were…as receptive as I thought you were."

She'd be lying if she didn't admit that she'd been thinking about him since he arrived in New York to make himself a presence at the Sher. Not only was he beguiling, but also he had a depth and a frankness that she was very attracted to. At this point in her life, she didn't need superficial encounters. And the way he asked her what kind of massage she liked or how he always held the door open were tiny moves that spoke volumes to her. But feeling good from the actions of a man, no matter how engaging and attentive he was, wasn't in her plans. Spontaneous kissing wasn't on the itinerary, either. And, most importantly, not with her boss! Her boss! She needed to be oh so careful that nothing got in the way of her big opportunity. To kiss him was to tempt the fates. "Yes, I was receptive, I just wanted to be clear that I don't think that qualified as dating."

"You don't pull any punches, do you, Esme? You tell it like it is."

"I can't afford not to. Whoever started it… Oh, wait, I mean that was you, which isn't to say that it wasn't lovely."

"And you want to agree that we'll never let anything like that happen again?"

"Right, I mean we're work partners now and maybe just being here in Stockholm in the snow was a little romantic." Well, actually, very romantic.

"Got it. Pact. We're coworkers and that's all we should ever be."

"Good, I just wouldn't want you to misunderstand my willingness to… When you kissed me and…" Then she yanked his hand to stop walking. And turned herself toward him, got up on her tippy toes and kissed him again. Was she crazy? Just after they'd made big proclamations that they weren't going to kiss again? His mouth felt so amazing that she couldn't help herself, kissing him in short presses. Soon followed by a not-so-short one that involved their tongues. That involved his tongue rolling along hers. Their mouths sealing to each other. Kisses that were hypnotizing, making sparks ignite that heated her on the inside. How could she feel so hot in the snow? "Oh, no." She stopped abruptly.

"Okay, that was definitely you, right?"

"I'm sorry. That really, really was the last time." The words came out of her mouth but she didn't mean them. She did want it to happen again. Right there on the street, or in more private quarters. She couldn't be blamed, could she? Those kisses were a kind of wake-up that made a person want more. Like a lifetime's worth, perhaps. Although she wouldn't do it again. She bore her eyes into his and told him so without words. His eyes were glassy as he returned the stare. With desire. His mere gaze sent blood coursing through her. This trip was quickly becoming very complicated.

When they came in from the cold and entered the hotel, a few people sat at the tables and chairs in the lobby as the front desk manager greeted them. "May I send up some champagne?"

Esme didn't ask Jackson before answering, *"Nej, tack."*

Things had become awkward and she just

wanted to get away from him at this point to collect herself and regroup.

Jackson argued, "Not so fast. Can you send me up a plate of meatballs and potatoes?" he asked the manager. "What about you, Esme? We only ate leaves at the spa. Aren't you hungry?"

"Nothing for me. I'm ready for bed." Although she certainly took note that he'd asked whether she was hungry. Someone concerned if she'd had enough to eat. Hmm. How nice that was.

They ducked into the elevator. Exiting on their floor, they walked down the quiet and softly lit corridor until they reached their rooms, which were across from each other.

Based on those kisses that they equally participated in, Esme sensed that she'd only need to invite him in as a method of communicating that she wanted to take things further. On one hand, she did. Desperately, as a matter of fact. She was so drawn to him and imagined little snippets of what could be. How his kisses might land on her neck. How his big hands might feel on her bare skin. Would they be rough or gentle? Would they feel hot like his tongue?

She'd been intimate with a few men. A couple of encounters were one-nighters and a few more lasted for a couple of months until it was clear there was nothing going on to warrant continuing to see each other. She knew that she'd never been made love to in a way that stirred her center. That would make her replay the encounters in a dreamy haze for days afterward. The kind that touched all the way down. And the scary thing was, she was certain that would all change if she shared a bed with Jackson. Like he had all of that in him just waiting to burst up. The thought set off screaming red warning signals that taking things any further with him would put her in emotional danger. Not to mention the possible jeopardy of her career.

So, it was in great haste that she tapped the key card to her room, said a quick good-night over her shoulder and dashed through the door, waiting to hear the definitive click of the lock behind her before she could lean back against the wall and let out a sigh that was relief mixed with disappointment. Because maybe, just maybe, she had actually met someone who was showing her that what she thought she had all figured out, that living her life alone was the best solution, might not be so. This was new information. And unwelcome at that.

On the plane to Oaxaca, Esme and Jackson were served a lavish Mexican breakfast of eggs and chorizo topped with red salsa and cheese, accompanied by sweet bread rolls called *conchas* and spice-laden coffee. He'd ordered room service last night yet they both ate heartily. It was so yummy they didn't talk for a few minutes; all they could do was sensually indulge. More sensuality. His kisses at night and great food in the morning. She could hardly decide which was more decadent. Oh, that wasn't true. She knew which. Though she hadn't had much of that deliciousness in her life.

Lying in her Stockholm hotel bed last night, she'd felt everything change. That steely-eyed future she envisioned became not enough. She'd decided long ago against men and coupledom. That she wasn't going to devote all of her resources to someone else. There'd been enough of that. Especially when her journey had taught her that she could expect nothing in return. She was not going to spend her life repeating the same pattern. Of people taking but not giving. As a result, she'd never been in a relationship as she only seemed to attract the wrong sort of man. Until now.

Was it the way Jackson kissed her that was so earthshaking? A give-and-take kind of exchange unlike anything she'd ever felt before? Whatever the provocation, her mental fog lifted and she saw the sky in a whole new way. How honest she and Jackson were with each other about their pasts and about how those pasts colored their lives now. There was something similar about their fear of betrayal, of trust, a trait hardened by their circumstances. She had this strange instinct that she could tell him anything and that he'd understand, and that she wanted to tell him everything. She had friends but she tended to keep things closer to the vest. When a child learns that information from one person can be used against another, it's training to keep their intimacies to themselves.

Now here, on this whirlwind trip with Jackson, she realized, and strangely for the very first time, that she was walking a very lonely road. It was a choice. And that there might be another one. A scarier one. But one that might have untold rewards that she'd never dared to dream of. Where someone wanted to know if she was hungry, and two people shared their ups and downs, hiked through the hills and valleys of a lifetime holding hands. It was overwhelming to consider what she'd never allowed herself before.

Once they finally slowed down on their gigantic plates of food, Jackson said, "I have to admit that I felt pretty good after that massage." His out-of-the-blue comment made her smile from ear to ear. Half in victory that she was getting him to understand the benefits of spa and half because it was so cute that he was admitting it to her as if he couldn't believe it himself. "Maybe my personal methods of self-care could use a makeover just like the Sher."

"Remind me again, what are those?"

"Barriers to ever being close to someone. Then there's living in corporate hotels so as to call no place home, spending as much time alone as possible, burying myself in work, always a screen in front of me, not getting fresh air. I think in your parlance you'd say I was *disconnecting* as best I could."

"Ooh, very good. Disconnecting."

He bowed his head as if accepting the accolade. "Thank you."

He reached over to steal an orange slice from her plate without asking. The familiarity in that made her heart ding though she pretended to protest with, "Hey!"

It was good that they weren't hashing over the snowflakes and hot sparks of last night. They'd talked it through, agreed it was a mistake. Now they were back to getting to know each other as colleagues with some kind of kindred spirits that would enhance their professional relationship. A good decision. No problem. If only she believed that herself. Because her insides were definitely replaying what had transpired.

"I told you," he continued, "my parents didn't value, or even understand, self-care. They worked day and night, coexisting in a world of numbers and flow charts and global predictions."

"And you've followed in their footsteps."

"I thought I needed more. Romance. Rapture. Exaltation. My one attempt to rebel was to marry a sparkly person who turned out to be made of smoke and mirrors. And now that's how I regard most everyone. As if I suspect them of something. In fact, after the whole debacle with Livia I did something I'll always regret."

"What's that?"

He hesitated before he committed to saying, "I fired the accountant who discovered that funds were missing from some accounts."

"He or she was who brought it to your attention?"

"Tom, yeah. I fired him in what I told myself was an abundance of caution. I found out later that he'd only reported on those accounts, he'd never had any access to them like Livia had."

"Couldn't you have hired him back?"

"He rightly didn't want to work for someone who thought that little of him."

"That's a lot to carry. You might want to unload some of this."

"What does that mean?"

"See a therapist, read a book about letting go and forgiving yourself. Hoping for an honest wife wasn't so much to ask for, or expect." Her words hung in the air. "Let's do some breathing. Inhale through your nose…"

He followed along but she could tell he was contemplating what she'd said. Finally he changed the subject to, "What's in store for me in Mexico?"

She shifted. "Cozumel and Luis's spa is

very specialized. That's what I have in mind for the Sher."

"Give me a preview."

"I know so many spas with full menus of skin and bodywork. New York is obviously one of the magnets in the world for the finest in skin care. So what if we eliminated that entirely from our menu?"

"Huh?"

"Don't compete with those famed skin care salons. Focus only on certain kinds of bodywork. And build a reputation on that. Let's be the best at specific modalities. I want to show you what Cozumel and Luis are doing. That's what I'd like to model us on."

She could see his wheels turning. He was the boss, after all. That was okay. She wanted them to have a partnership where they both had a vested interest in the Sher's success. She'd need his approval. This was already a victory for her, being heard, allowed to show him her vision. His snow-flurry kisses, buried agonies of his past and her questions about being alone would all fall to the wayside. She hoped.

CHAPTER SEVEN

SECRETLY, JACKSON'S GUT was doing push-ups while he tried to keep his face neutral. He was all but sitting on his hands to resist the temptation to get another taste of what he'd gorged on last night. Esme's lips. He would never recover from those kisses that were the sweetest nectar he'd ever tasted. Not to mention the soft skin of her face and neck that his fingers had the good fortune to have stroked. All of which was very logically discussed and decided against, the same as an ill-advised business decision. Of course, the trouble was that he'd spent the entire night tossing and turning on those pale yellow Swedish sheets in bed alone with very contradictory thoughts.

"*Bienvenidos* to Oaxaca International Airport," the pilot announced over the sound system after they'd touched ground back on the North American continent. Jackson looked out the window at open sky and mountainous terrain, so very different than the Swedish vistas they'd arrived from.

"I hope you find this a special visit," Esme turned to say.

A driver took them a bit outside of Oaxaca City to reach Spa Bajo el Sol, or Spa under the Sun. When they arrived, Esme couldn't wait and flung the door open to bound out of the car and greet a man and a woman who were seemingly waiting for them outside the entrance in front of a tiled fountain with a bountiful spray of almost blue water. Esme ran toward them calling out, "Cozumel! Luis!" When she reached them, the three exchanged hugs. Esme turned to extend a hand to Jackson and bring him into the circle with the Aguilars. "This is Jackson Finn, who I told you about."

"Hola," Cozumel greeted him. "Thank you for having an interest in the work we do here."

"With Esme's help I'm only just beginning to understand the scope of what spa really means." He brought forward a hand to shake, which Cozumel and Luis ignored, both bringing him into an awkward hug of their own.

After they disentangled, Cozumel said, "Here at Bajo el Sol we focus on ancient work regarding fertility and both male and female reproductive health. What we do is unique. We're blessed that guests have found us and have spread the word about our treatments."

Esme said to Jackson, "See, that's what I'm talking about. Rather than a general spa, they specialize and draw a clientele from all over the world."

"This is a place of love. Our bodies. Our bellies. Our babies."

"You must be hungry and thirsty after your journey," Luis said. "Let me show you to your casita." Esme had told Jackson that while Bajo el Sol wasn't a hotel spa, they did keep some accommodations for friends and family, and guests having sensitive treatments. They'd be staying in one of the small houses that faced out to a view of groves and mountains. The sunny skies and blustery breezes were quite a change from Sweden.

"Remind me, Luis," Esme asked as they walked toward the horizon, "what year did you establish the spa?"

"It's twenty-five years already." They followed him to the casita he pointed to. "The adobe walls of the buildings help keep the interior cool in summer and warm in winter. Come in." The small house was furnished and decorated with traditional Mexican design, bold colors in a rustic setting. Two bedrooms shared a bathroom.

"This is lovely."

"We are closed for the evening and there are no other overnight guests so you have the run of the property. Drop off your bags and then join us in the kitchen. It's the back door in the main house, or did you remember that, Esme?"

She'd told Jackson that she'd worked here for two years, staying in a spare room in the house, and credited Cozumel and Luis with teaching her many valuable lessons about both operations and treatments. "Oh, I remember the kitchen. How could I ever forget your Oaxacan cooking? Jackson, you're going to love Luis's food."

"As long as there's no kale."

They did as Luis suggested and freshened up in the casita, putting on comfortable clothes to suit the mild weather. Jackson had taken Esme's advice during that sexy phone call before they left and had packed lightweight clothes and canvas shoes. Esme looked angelic in a loose white dress.

In the large, open kitchen, Luis was stirring a huge cauldron over a fire, and everywhere Jackson turned there were pots and utensils that looked to be centuries old. "We have some *antojitos* ready," Cozumel said and pointed to the counter where an appetizer was sitting invitingly on a platter painted with the sun and moon around the rim. Beside it was a glass pitcher filled with a pale green drink. "These are *garnachas*," Luis said.

Cozumel jumped in with, "Small tortillas topped with shredded meat."

"And pickled cabbage," Luis added.

"And, to drink." Cozumel gestured to the pitcher.

Luis said, "That's a melon *liquado*."

They helped themselves to a more than ample snack. "Oh, my goodness," Jackson couldn't help but extoll, "these are divine."

After Luis attempted to stuff their faces into oblivion merely on appetizers, Esme wanted to go back to the casita before the main course. She plopped herself down on the couch. "I'm exhausted. I didn't sleep on the flight. I think I have jet lag."

"New York to Sweden to Mexico in just a few days can cause that." He cracked open the cap of a water bottle from the counter and handed it to her. "Drink."

"Maybe I'll take a little nap."

"Nope. The best thing is to get on Mexican time. Let's sit outside in the sun. That helps me sometimes."

"Mr. Finn, do I actually detect some knowledge about taking care of yourself?"

"Don't tell anyone." He put one finger up to his mouth for a shush. "I travel a lot. It's more like self-preservation." He stretched out an arm to pull her off of the couch.

They lay on the patio loungers that were on the patio. Esme lifting her face to the sun was unspeakably beautiful. After a while she said, "Hey, thanks for looking after me. I do feel better."

His mind was everywhere. How connected Cozumel and Luis were, practically finishing each other's sentences. Strange flashbacks about Livia, remembering the giddy feeling he had for a very short time in the beginning when he thought he was in love. How being a couple made him feel part of something he wanted and felt incomplete without. How it wasn't that his parents didn't care for each other, but they just didn't show it. For some reason they didn't think it needed expressing, or kindling, or romancing. In Livia, he was chasing that something different he thought he needed. Instead, all he came away with was hurt. And shame. Esme was right. If he was ever going to let go of the regret he carried in his body, he needed to let the shame go.

When they returned to the main house after it had gotten dark, Luis had finished preparing dinner. It was to be eaten under the stars at a table made from clear blue glass pieces that picked up bits of moonlight here and there. Just as Esme's hair did.

"When everybody thinks about Oaxacan cooking they think of our moles. There are many variations," Cozumel explained as she served Jackson a piece of grilled chicken onto which she ladled a dark sauce.

Luis jumped in with, "Mole contains dozens of ingredients and takes days to make. When Cozumel told me you were coming, I began this mole *negro* for you."

"You'll taste the subtle flavor of chocolate balanced with acidic tomatillos, nuts, tortillas, dried fruit, chili peppers. It's both savory and sweet."

Jackson took a bite and the richness and complexity of the sauce delighted his taste buds. "Thank you, Luis, this is beyond delicious."

Esme nodded emphatically in agreement.

Luis carried out a clay pot. "With it, we'll have black beans with epazote, an herb we farm here at the spa. We cook it with some onions and a little bit of bacon so it's herby but rich."

Next came a tray. "My goodness," Esme marveled. "This is enough food to feed New York City."

"*Tlayudas*, which are like our pizzas. We spread a tortilla with beans, *asiento*, which is pork lard, cheese and tasajo. Dried beef."

"And no kale whatsoever," Jackson said to no one.

After dinner Cozumel served them a small glass of mezcal, a spirit made from the agave plant, which had a smoky flavor. And a chocolate sampling on another beautiful plate, this one painted with sunflowers. "Chocolate is very important to us. It's used for all occasions and rituals. You'll see tomorrow we even use it in the spa."

"Cozumel, what treatments will we show Jackson?"

"I have a longtime client, Payaan, who I've seen through her fertility issues. She's willing to have you observe our work together. Tomorrow, we do demonstrations. Tonight, we rest. Now, go sit by the firepit, take the mezcal and the chocolate with you and just be. Surrender to the moon." It was as if Cozumel knew him, knew that her simple instruction wasn't an easy one for him to follow.

Sitting on one of the circular stone benches that rounded the firepit, they quietly nibbled the chocolate and watched the orange flames tickle the night. It wasn't just the physical connection between them he couldn't stop thinking about. It was that all of his pronouncements and decrees about never getting close to a woman were melting like snowflakes in the firepit. He'd be all business with Esme, like they'd agreed. Yet his heart would know that it was her who had cracked his hard shell, giving him an inkling that being with someone heart, body and soul might be worth the risk of his greatest fear coming true, that he'd be betrayed again.

Eventually, he stood. "After such a wonderful meal, I think I'm the one who is going to fall asleep right here if we don't get to the casita." They got up and strolled under the moonlight and stars to their little house.

"Hard to believe we began our day in Stockholm."

"Let's go to bed." It was strange the way that came out of his mouth. As if they were a longtime married couple who always retired to bed together. It just came out that way. He surely wasn't speaking from personal experience. He and Livia had no bedtime ritual. He often stayed awake much later than she did, communicating with the rest of the world from his computer, some people beginning their workdays, some at the end. Time had no particular meaning to him and he hadn't considered it that much until this moment, when it seemed as if he and Esme and the black night sky were part of something connected, and last night in Stockholm they were part of something else. But perhaps his lofty musings were just those snowy kisses doing the talking.

"Here we are," Esme stated the obvious when they stepped into the casita and headed to the bedrooms.

His best bet would have been to walk straight into his room and close the door.

Which he succeeded at. Except for one tiny detour. And that was over to Esme's face to give her lovely cheek just a peck of a good-night kiss.

Okay, he almost succeeded in that scenario, too. The kiss ended up on her sumptuous lips, which tasted like chocolate. And it was decidedly more than a peck.

"That kiss was your doing, right?" Esme pointed at him and played tough guy, but with a twitch of a smile.

"Yes. Not you. Me."

"Just checking." She entered her bedroom and shut the door, leaving him standing in the divide between the two rooms, frozen, stunned.

"Mayan abdominal massage, which is part of healing practices called *sobada*, has been around since Mesoamerican times," Cozumel told Jackson the next morning as they walked to the open-air massage plaza with its tent-like roof. A massage table was dressed with clean linens and a wooden cabinet with open doors displayed shelves of towels and products used for treatments. A small woman sat on the table under the shade. "Payaan, these are my friends Esme and Jackson who I told you about."

She made eye contact with them. Esme considered that it was very open of the woman to allow her and Jackson to observe her treatment. As if on cue, Payaan ran her palm across her belly.

Esme asked her, "Can I help you lie down?" She put out her hand and Payaan took it to help herself into position.

"We're being extra careful with Payaan. Although she has one beautiful daughter, six years old if I remember correctly," Cozumel said, to which Payaan nodded, "she's having trouble holding another pregnancy. We're going to try some techniques that have been used for centuries to aid in fertility."

"Gracias," the otherwise quiet Payaan whispered.

Cozumel began with a singsong chant in Spanish, blessing the elements that had joined them for today's journey. While she did that, she gently stroked Payaan's left arm from finger to shoulder and then her right. She did the same up the length of each leg from foot to hip. She rolled Payaan's skirt down from the waist, exposing the smooth brown skin of her abdomen, the soft center of her. "We'll set our intention to pour love into Payaan's belly, to send her the sun and the moon, water and fire."

"I will." Esme closed her eyes and brought those very images to mind, trying to use her own energy to penetrate into Payaan. She imagined her spirit traveling into the woman with every exhale. Afterward, she opened her eyes and shifted her gaze to Jackson. She didn't imagine he'd be spiritually trying to move his life force but nonetheless he was stilled by the uniqueness of the moment. And, after all, that's why they were there, to show him how transformative this specific care could be. Esme had this one chance to affect Payaan's reproductive health because tomorrow they'd be gone, and Cozumel would be on to her next client.

Cozumel washed her hands with the collected rainwater she poured from a pitcher, and dried them on a fluffy towel. She rubbed her palms together to warm them and then placed both down on Payaan's belly.

"Join me, Esme. If that's all right, Payaan." She nodded. Esme followed Cozumel in washing and drying her hands, warming them with friction and then placing them onto Payaan. The four hands moved to gently press into her belly, feeling for information. "Payaan, I sense some movement in you. Perhaps you are ovulating, either today or within the next couple of days." She began gently lifting and gliding along Payaan's stomach, moving with her fingertips in an outward circle. Esme did the same.

To Jackson, Esme explained, "With *sobada* techniques we can sometimes guide the uterus into the optimal position in the lower pelvis."

"How?" he asked simply. Esme was happy that he was taking an interest. She had wondered how he would feel about coming to Oaxaca to a spa that concerned itself mainly with fertility. But he seemed to understand that this was a very specialized practice, and Cozumel a very gifted practitioner.

"We can increase circulation to the area and break up blockage. That brings a better flow of oxygen and relieves stagnation."

"Esme has a beautiful touch," Cozumel said to Jackson. "She always has. She was born with it." Jackson caught Esme's eyes and smiled sweetly with what looked like pride. She all but blushed in return. A moment not lost on Cozumel.

No one but Esme knew the surprising gift of Jackson's touch. When he'd embraced her during those kisses in Stockholm. Even his impromptu palm at the small of her back when going through the airport was hypnotizing. His big hands were sure and powerful, teeming with energy waves. She was trying very hard to pretend that she didn't crave more.

Esme said, "The menu here can help with other ailments and maladies as well such as endometriosis, blocked tubes, fibroids, cysts, painful menstrual cramps, prostate health for men. And prenatal care, to ensure the mother and baby are comfortable and breathing easily."

They were quiet for the rest of the treatment, the rustling breeze their only sound. Upon completion of the session, Cozumel said, "Now we'll bring closure to our work together. That's part of the healing. We'll anoint Payaan's belly with cocoa oil and wrap her in a rebozo, a ceremonial shawl." Esme pulled the needed items from the cabinet.

After the session they reviewed. "I could

see Payaan respond to you, Esme. You were a talented novice and you've become skilled in and out of the treatment room. I wish I could bring you back permanently. I'm too busy to take on all of the requests I get. Plus, my spa director, Itza, will herself soon take a maternity leave to birth her own baby and she hasn't decided if and when she'll return."

"My honor." Esme appreciated the praise. It was a transformative two years she'd spent here, learning from Cozumel and gaining the confidence her own parents failed to give her. Poignant that she was back here during this turning point in her life. In more ways than one, as she was here with this extraordinary man who was making her question all that she'd held sacred.

With the demonstration completed, Cozumel suggested Esme show Jackson the mud therapy. They changed into swimsuits and headed to the mud pavilion, another outdoor space on the property. As he walked a few paces ahead of her, Esme couldn't help admiring Jackson's sturdy back, his skin glistening in the late-afternoon glow. When they were in session with Cozumel, it was a thrill that he was so interested in the work that was done here. To understand this was to understand her. She'd never met anyone outside of the spa industry who had.

"Have you ever used a mud pool? We coat ourselves in the wet clay mud and then we sit out in the sun to let it dry. After that we rub it off, and then rinse with geothermal mineral water, which is one of nature's greatest detoxifiers."

Esme used hands full of clay from the well to completely cover one arm in a thin layer to show Jackson, who was quick to follow. "Slimy."

"It's food for your skin. The paste will nourish."

"Does my skin need nourishing?" he asked, getting used to the sensation and applying the clay to his chest.

"Yes, this is incredible restoration for your skin, another natural remedy that's been around for centuries. It stimulates your skin function. Did you know that skin is the body's largest organ?"

"I didn't even know that skin was an organ."

"The mud pulls out the impurities so they don't enter your bloodstream. It balances the skin, which can even have a sedative effect."

"And I didn't know that my skin needed sedation, either."

"Oh, that's a little thick on your chest. Let me." She reached out with a flat palm to spread out the too-heavy layer he had created. He took a quick intake of breath, making her realize that her hands were having an effect on him.

Just as his chest was having an effect on her hands. His solid muscles and skin so warm it was bringing the mud to a perfect temperature.

They looked at each other, a silent conversation that went long past clay. She wondered about being here in Mexico, about Jackson's dark eyes, heated skin and the penetrating feeling that she had been missing out on something central to the meaning of life.

"Do you want me to do your back?"

"Please."

He turned around, and it was almost painful not to be able to see his face. She dutifully coated his back, whispering in his ear from behind, "It's easier when there's someone to help, isn't it?"

"I can see that now."

Once she'd applied the mud to the curves and planes of his extremely attractive back, he circled around. "My turn." It was a statement not an inquiry. She gave him access and his hands were indeed sent from heaven as they applied the clay to her shoulder blades, vibrating through her. In fact, she had to pull away because she was starting to feel so turned on and needed to put herself in check.

Fully coated, they lay on wooden reclining chairs. After a quiet time breathing the clean air and lost in thought she said, "Thank you for your suggestions yesterday. You really helped me with my jet lag."

"I'm glad to hear." He'd done something for her, and they both valued that more than she could express.

After a while it was time to begin sloughing the mud off. They moved to the cavelike rock formation where the spouts of showers awaited. "It's best if you rub as much as you can while it's still dry so there's less thickness to wash off. See?" She vigorously rubbed one area of her arm, watching the now-powdery clay fall from her skin. He did the same. Then they turned on the showers and let the rest of the mud glide down their bodies and swirl into the drain. "We'll finish washing up at the casita." Their time here was coming to a close. Tonight they were headed out on a late flight to Bangkok, onto the next, and last, spa.

CHAPTER EIGHT

JACKSON TURNED ON the casita's outdoor shower with its privacy and unforgettable mountain view so they could finish getting the mud off. He took a mental snapshot as he would remember this place for the rest of his life. This whole trip had already been an unexpected odyssey. What he was learning about himself as well as spa. He slipped off his still-muddy swim trunks and tossed them into the woven laundry hamper provided. Naked, he turned to Esme, aware that removing the small piece of fabric from his body actually presented a dilemma. He could tell that he'd aroused her by applying the mud, the way they'd talked to each other with their hands instead of words. And he certainly couldn't hide the physical effect she'd had on him. Was she comfortable being nude around him? There was no choice but to find out. She removed her bathing suit and he tried to keep from gawking at the parts of her he hadn't seen bare. Sort of. He was overwhelmed with a desire for the freedom, to take the action that his heart so wanted.

Unable to not, he guided them both under the showerhead and he took her face in his hands. He kissed her lips, lightly, then again until each kiss was slower than the last. He put his arms around her, hands stroking up the length of her back. The more mud that washed off, the softer she felt. He held her to him closely but not tight, just taking in the totality of the moment. Here, with her. It almost didn't seem real, this new life he'd stepped into the moment he returned to the Sher after his long absence. It was only the job of washing the mud off of her body that kept him grounded on earth. Otherwise, he might have floated up into the white clouds that dotted the bright blue sky.

"We're doing it again." He felt it necessary to label the moment, to make sure he wasn't coercing her.

"I want to make love with you, Jackson. Just once. We can handle that, can't we? We know what we're doing."

"I've wanted you every moment of every day since I came into the Sher." He kissed the lips that were glistening wet from the shower. "Yes, once, and only once, then we'll never taste the danger again." He had to have her. A promise of only once made sense. Then, with their itches scratched, they'd go on to a long and prosperous partnership. It would be a matter of will that they were both capable of.

He began wide swipes with his hands across her sides and lower, washing away every speck of mud until impulse had him move to the front of her. His hands held her breasts before his eyes did, round, firm, sized for a precious handful. The hiss of his inhale let her know she had his rapt attention. He'd dare not reach down between her thighs, not yet anyway. They had until late night to board their flight to Bangkok. He was not going to rush this moment that they promised would be a one-time memory. He knew it would be his greatest treasure, forever.

His lips trailed to her neck and when he moved her wet hair aside to kiss and nip there, she let out a small moan of pleasure that gushed through him. His mouth traveled to kiss those inviting breasts, first with wisps down the outer side of one, then the other. Then his mouth longed for, and found, a nipple which he tickled with the tip of his tongue at least a thousand times. When his teeth returned to her throat, her head fell back to receive him again.

"Jackson," she barely murmured, "that feels so good."

"Thank you for telling me so." He did love making love even though he'd previously compartmentalized it as recreation with no emotional involvement. He'd barely witnessed any physical contact between his parents, who were always walking out the door to a meeting or some such. His father never sat him down and talked to him about anatomy or contraception, leaving that to the little bit of health education that was taught in schools. Nor did anyone ever talk to him about how to treat women. Gentlemanly behavior, yes, but not intimacy matters such as consent and consequences and attachments. He was left on his own with all of that. Perhaps a little more information in that regard might have helped him recognize who not to marry.

But by about age sixteen, when he was expected to participate in the family business, he found himself at functions and charity events where well-to-do women who were twice his age took interest in him and introduced him to sexuality. To some wild escapades, in fact. For example, making love on the rooftop of a forty-story building in Manhattan at two o'clock in the morning. Through being with older women who easily communicated their proclivities and needs better than less experienced younger women, he learned a valuable lesson. That sex was much more pleasurable to him if it was equally pleasurable to the woman he was with. He made up his mind to become a skilled and perceptive lover.

Those women, some married or divorced or career-focused, were as careful as he was not to form any taboo emotional involvements. He broke no hearts nor had his heart broken until Livia, who swindled him into thinking they *had it all*—the business, a passionate love and a genuine connection. How gullible he'd been, perhaps starved after all of those meaningless encounters with other women and the chilly home he grew up in.

Now it was Esme who was presenting him with a test to all of his rules and regulations. He felt something toward her that with Livia was only a facade. The pulling in his soul that told him he might want to actually be with her, to be a melded couple that moved through life together. *Together* together. Which was an unsafe place for him to be. He couldn't have his heart broken again. All of this traveling with Esme, seeing things as if through only one lens, natural partners in every sense of the word, was making him reconsider what he'd resigned to, whether he wanted to or not. He really didn't mean for this closeness to be developing between them, yet it was. Like destiny. Like fate.

His mouth captured hers again to merge under the shower into their fullest, most urgent kisses yet. She wrapped her arms around his neck and he ran his hands along the expanse, from her shoulder to her elbows to her wrists.

"Yes," she moaned. "Oh, heavens, yes."

A smile cracked his lips as his hand trailed down her side and slipped between her legs. She gasped. He held her in the palm of his hand, letting her sex press against it, finding what was good. She buried her face in his neck and her slow train of breath coaxed him to continue. His fingers started a gentle motion and found a groove for her, so he didn't vary it either in speed or in pressure, instead letting her do the moving against his hand, tuning it to her own comfort and pleasure. He himself became rock-hard in the doing. Once she was close to going over the edge, he added kisses to her décolletage until her back arched then she shattered into his hand with a long cry out.

He murmured into her ear, "Magnificent."

After sufficiently washing each other with soapy hands, he shut off the tap and handed her a big fluffy towel in the terra cotta color that was part of the spa's signature logo. "Jackson, I have to tell you something."

"Okay, please do." What did she have on her mind? Even though she'd said she wanted to make love, he wouldn't go any further if she had any hesitations.

"I've never…" Oh, was she going to tell him that she was a virgin? She'd mentioned dating although not having ever been in a serious relationship. He'd imagined that she'd had sex before. Not that he would have minded being her first as she seemed to be enjoying herself so far.

"Yes?" he encouraged her.

"I've never had real lovemaking before. The men I've been with were only interested in their own pleasure, and in achieving it as quickly as possible."

He brushed her hair from her face and smiled with what he hoped was reassurance. "Shall we change that?"

"I think we already have. The way you made my body quake just now was a first for me. I'm sorry I don't have experience pleasing a man, either. Will you tell me what feels arousing to you?"

"I will." He let her lead him into the casita and straight into the bed that had been designated as hers. She laid her naked body in the center of it. "I'll be right back," he said, remembering that he needed to grab protection from his luggage. He dashed into the other bedroom and back as quickly as he could. Then he climbed onto the bed, kissing and caressing her shapely legs along the way.

Hours passed although it seemed like days as he and Esme gave and received. Learning and taking chances. Bringing each other to unimaginable bliss. Finding themselves in positions that were not only unfamiliar to Esme, but were to Jackson as well. While he'd had some profound sexual encounters, ones that he revisited in his mind even years after the fact, those too, were nothing compared to what he shared with Esme in a wooden bed in Mexico with the scent of dirt and flowers wafting in and out of the open windows. Finding out what brought Esme to ecstasy was the most erotic experience he'd ever had. She was more than capable of igniting him without needing instruction. They rose and fell, danced and shook, penetrated, twisted, grasped, held and joined over and over and over again.

After the visit to the heavens and back with Jackson, Esme could see out the bedroom window that dusk was beginning to settle, which meant they only had a few hours left until they departed for Thailand. There was one more thing that she wanted to do before they left Spa Bajo el Sol, a place of such importance to her. Although it wasn't easy, she dislodged herself from Jackson's enveloping embrace and got out of bed. She turned to him. "Come on."

"Where are we going?"

They threw on some clothes and wandered into the main house where, no surprise, Luis was hard at work in the kitchen chopping vegetables. "Do you want to show Jackson where you stayed when you were here?"

"That's exactly where I was headed."

"Take a look at the photos we put up."

Easily remembering her way, she took Jackson's hand and led him through the common areas of the big house to the other side where the bedrooms were. Her old digs were through the farthest door on the left. The room was decorated as all of the house was, with traditional Mexican styling and open windows. A single-sized bed had a colorful blanket and pillows.

"This is it. This is where I slept when I worked here."

Jackson looked around. "Small, but I'm sure you had everything you needed." He noticed a gallery of photos mounted on the far wall and he moved to check them out. He pointed to one and beckoned her over. "Oh, my goodness."

As soon as she spotted the photo he was referring to, she put her hand over her mouth with a giggle. "Yup. Yours truly."

In the photo she was standing behind a seated Luis, her hands on his shoulders giving him a shoulder massage. Cozumel stood beside, squeezing oil from a bottle onto him, the three of them laughing uproariously. Esme even recalled that exact moment. The validation she'd gained here was invaluable to her.

Jackson actually reached out and touched Esme's face in the photo. "What a little beauty you are. How old were you here?"

"Let's see. I'm thirty-two now, so I was twenty-two."

She glanced at the other photos on the wall. They were of other young practitioners the spa had employed over the years, happy faces of every race, creed and color. Cozumel and Luis made it a habit to employ industry workers seeking experience. She used to joke that it was because they had no children of their own.

"You were just a babe." Jackson stayed focused on her picture.

"Yeah, but I was licensed by then."

"Could you teach me a little bit about how to give a massage? I mean, obviously it would take years to develop the skills you have, but would you show me how to do something simple?"

"Why?"

"It would be such a gift to make people feel transformed the way you do."

Oh, he'd made her feel plenty good just a while ago in the casita. What Jackson did to her very being. He lifted her to the spirits, taking her to a celestial high. It was a lifetime's worth of sensual information in only one encounter. Besides him having some sort of mystical skill at knowing her body, they had a desperation for each other that had to be fulfilled. Still, she'd bet he'd have a pretty fine touch for those basic massage strokes.

"Okay. Lie down face down on the bed." He stretched his gorgeous body out and she knelt at his side. "Even though you claimed you weren't that impressed with the massage in Stockholm, what do you remember about it?"

"That massage therapist was intense. I didn't like the way he looked at you."

"What? I mean about the work he did. How did he look at me?"

"Like you were prey."

"I doubt that." She'd barely paid attention to him, she was so busy trying to make sure Jackson had a positive session.

He considered her words, seeming to replay the session in his mind. "Well, in any case, I got a bad vibe from him."

"How about his skills?"

"He had some good moves."

"Name one."

"His palms along the sides of my torso. It was a kind of lengthening that was pleasant."

"Like this?" Esme demonstrated on Jackson's body. "It's called effleurage."

"Yeah. Can I try it on you?" The man who started off saying he didn't value touch wanted to practice some technique. Everything but everything seemed to be changing in the winds.

She had to admit this was fun. And of all places, in the house where she'd spent two years learning and growing. She gave Jackson a gentle push to make room for her on the bed and then he was the one to kneel beside her. He rapidly glided his hands along her torso.

"Okay, first of all you've got to slow that down." He attempted again but this time he was using the tips of his fingers. "Not with your fingers, use your palms."

She let him try a few more times, offering pointers with each attempt.

"This isn't easy."

"You see what we mean if someone has a particularly good touch. It takes hundreds of hours to master a protocol."

He kept trying, genuinely paying attention to her tutorial and improving with every stroke.

"That's nice, Jackson. What you have to do is learn from my body's response. Am I melding into your hand or are my muscles resisting?" He'd certainly gotten that one right at the casita. Was she really never going to have that with him again?

"It's so much more complicated than it looks."

"It is at that." Were they still talking about massage?

Eventually, they ended up lying next to each other on their backs, holding hands and staring at the ceiling, the sky outside now pitch-black. They might have slept there all night.

However, they had a plane to catch.

"Welcome to Thailand," Esme said, peeling her gaze away from the airplane window after she'd watched their descent into Bangkok. It had been a couple of years since she'd been in the country and she was looking forward to showing Jackson about traditions that particularly resonated with her.

She was also glad to be seeing Hathai Sitwat, owner of the world-renowned Spa

Malee, which translated as *flower spa*. In fact, as soon as they made their way off the plane and to the baggage claim area, their host was there waiting for them. She was a curvy woman with lush black hair, wearing a vibrant print dress. After all the hellos and introductions Hathai said to Jackson, "I visited the Sher when I was last in New York. It's a magnificent building."

"Thank you. It meant a lot to my parents."

"Precious gifts," she added, "things that were important to family that came before us." Given that most of what Esme remembered from her parents was their selfishness, she could only raise her eyebrows at Jackson. He seemed to understand her with a reassuring single nod. Lack of modeling healthy and caring relationships was, unfortunately, a childhood similarity that they shared at this point.

They took in the sights and sounds as their host drove them through a very lively and traffic-congested Bangkok. Hathai insisted that they stay at her house while they were in town. After turning down a street here and another there, Hathai entered the gate codes to access the front driveway, which was redolent with many colors of plants and flowers. Her home itself was a natural paradise.

Esme said, "This is incredible."

"I used to live in a high-rise apartment right by the spa," she explained. "It became unsustainable to never have quiet, to not hear a bird chirp. It was important for me to make the best use of my off time as possible."

"Yet you're still in the city."

"The best of both worlds. While I wait for grandchildren." Hathai was divorced with two grown sons. Had Jackson thought about children and grandchildren? Esme couldn't help but feel that this trip with him had opened her eyes. That it wasn't just a strategic move to win her the directorship at the Sher. That it was bringing her whole self into the light. And she wondered if it might be doing the same for him.

They entered the large house and Hathai showed them to their rooms. While they nibbled some snacks, Esme couldn't take her eyes off Jackson. She'd watched him sleep on the plane, taking her time to indulge in studying his face. In repose he looked different than when they'd made passionate love, the feral, urgent burn in his hungry eyes so untamed she thought she'd orgasm from just gazing into them. As exquisite as his big dark eyes were, there was art in them asleep as well. His face took on a calm that she didn't see while he was awake. With his lips slightly parted and the tiny whoosh of air that accompanied every exhale, he was a sight not unlike one of the world's wonders.

She hadn't slept on the flight again, and was moving forward on fumes. That and the memory of the lovemaking she'd never forget. Esme had had sex with a few men, slipping out of bed when they were done, out the door before morning as she let her actions speak for her. That she was done. Although that kind of conduct would now forever be in question should she ever again think to have unsatisfying relations with anyone else, so mind-altering was her interlude with Jackson.

Her body quivered just thinking about it now as she picked one of the slices of mango laid out on a plate. She slid a slippery, ripe and fragrant piece through her lips. How she wished she could slip half of the mango slice into Jackson's mouth while keeping the other side in hers and let them take slurpy bites of the juicy fruit until their mouths met in the middle.

Fantasy aside, she was well aware that she'd been walking on a dangerous wild side when she'd told Jackson that she wanted to make love with him. Once. Of course, in fairness to her, she had no way of knowing that doing so would be so spectacular it would send her into a daze she might never return from. How was she going to keep her vow that she was allowed a one-time exploration and nothing more? Her second bite of mango was more of a frustrated chomp.

The car ride was quick to Spa Malee. "Oh, this is so much like the Sher," Jackson noted to Hathai right away, given that the facility was located upstairs in a commercial building in a tony part of town. Also like the Sher, the spa had a separate entrance, an unassuming front door that was either opened by code or through a phone app. There was a small elevator, same as the Sher.

"Well, here's where the similarity ends," he said when the elevator door opened.

They exited to a small foyer, just big enough to hold a wooden bench topped with a couple of colorful cushions. Ambient sound of rainfall made the space seem farther from the street than it was. It was a perfect nook for someone who needed to sit for a moment as a transition. A side table had a pitcher of water with a stack of small metal cups. Art on the wall was traditional.

Esme said, "That's what I was saying about the Sher. The elevator opens to a sleek and exclusive New York property. Instead, I'd like clients to have a total magical paradise as soon as they arrive."

"Agreed," Jackson said.

After they stepped inside that door, Hathai gestured for them to remove their shoes and place them in the cubbies provided. Jackson's eyes began a three-hundred-and-sixty-degree survey of the lobby. "My, my," he uttered. Long panels of intricately carved wood adorned some of the walls. Others displayed paintings of the sun, the moon and stars. There were clusters of teakwood furniture with pillows covered in brilliant-colored silk fabrics, deep blues and bright yellows. Succulent green plants and fresh flowers were everywhere, creating the most delightful scent.

"The bare floor with all the wood and greenery gives it such an open look," he said.

Esme was glad Jackson could appreciate what a stunner this spa was.

Hathai said, "Let me take you in. When a

guest enters, we always greet them with tea or water." She discreetly pointed to a group of four women who were enjoying tea and laughter. "We have soundproof glazing on the windows so that in here we can disassociate from everything outside. And focus on being in a healing oasis."

"Hathai," Jackson asked, "when we were driving here through the city streets, and just like in New York, you see Thai massage businesses everywhere. With a sign outside listing prices, often much lower than for a spa. What is different about Spa Malee? I looked at your menu and of course you have high-end prices, appropriate for a luxury establishment like this."

"I think you answered your own question, Jackson." Hathai brought them to a semicirclular area of treatment rooms with more woods and silks. "In a street corner business, there are many people receiving massage in the same room. One next to the other. It's not at all private and it's not personalized for each guest. You could almost think of it as an assisted-movement class, comparable to yoga. Which isn't to say there's anything wrong with that. It shows us that this is medicine in Thailand, as it has been for thousands of years. It's part of a health care system for physical and energetic well-being. We advocate for those small studios. In fact, I own a dozen of them throughout the country where people who don't have the funds can receive treatment for free."

"What Hathai has established here," Esme added, "is the lavish secluded world of the day spa combined with a wellness center. That's what I want us to do at the Sher."

Ideas were solidifying in Esme's mind. Her concept for the spa she wanted. Something she'd mulled over for a long time but hadn't been in a position to execute. Bringing together all of these traditions from across the globe and creating a unique place like none other in New York. And the vision had now come to include Jackson, who had suddenly become her partner, her friend and one time, therefore, former lover. Everything seemed possible.

Hathai said, "We have chosen the finest of materials and furnishings for this spa, our flagship, and we hire only extensively experienced practitioners. Please," she invited and gestured with her arm to usher them into a treatment room.

"Welcome to utopia," Jackson said as he again took in the palatial surroundings.

"Please meet Aroon." A small man entered holding a big wooden bowl filled with flower petals and water. Esme knew right away that Hathai had called in this practitioner over another because he was small in stature, so that if he deemed to give Jackson the pressure technique of standing on his back, his weight wouldn't be a burden to bear.

Aroon put the flower bowl down on a small table that held a stack of white towels. He invited Jackson to take a seat in a cushioned throne-like chair. "At Spa Malee we have a special welcoming ritual to let you know how glad we are that you are here."

Again, Esme thought of what saying those words to a client in New York might mean, that level of welcome to someone who was sick or had an ongoing health issue, or to someone who didn't have a lot of touch in their life, or even to someone who was just burnt-out and needed personal attention.

Aroon set the bowl of water and flower petals down on the floor in front of Jackson, and dropped to his knees. Gently lifting one of Jackson's feet, he placed it in the water and began to use his fingers back and forth to brush one foot with the water, and then the other. Esme and Jackson smiled at each other, her knowing he was as grateful as she was to be sharing this together.

CHAPTER NINE

JACKSON WAS DEFINITELY in unfamiliar territory. Esme's world of the healing arts wasn't anything he'd ever contemplated. The people he'd met in the past few days were truly remarkable. While Aroon rubbed his feet with flower petals, strange as both a sensation and the unfamiliar setup of this tiny man kneeling at his feet, he couldn't take his eyes off Esme, who was observing the proceedings as if she was judging the accuracy. Making sure he was being attended to correctly. More of her caretaking instinct again.

In Oaxaca he'd had a chance to show her that she could be the one taken care of sometimes. He was still elated to reflect back on the satisfaction he felt from her cries of pleasure and her tight grip that begged him to continue whatever he was doing, a request he was only too delighted to oblige. He tried to close his eyes for a moment just to take in the sensation of the water at his feet, but it was too agonizing to take his gaze off her. Something was rising in him that he didn't ask for but had arrived nonetheless.

His feelings for her were long past employee and employer, no matter how many times he proclaimed that, and even past two single people who'd decided to give themselves to each other for one coupling. No, Jackson was starting to settle in to Esme being a permanent presence in his life. One he wanted to have around him all the time. He could see them as both business and life partners, could visualize a life in New York where he stayed put and they moved forward step after step after step into a reality he'd never expected, especially after his divorce. He blinked his eyes a few times to try to come back to the moment.

He was so glad that before they'd left Oaxaca, he'd asked her to teach him a tiny bit of her considerable repertoire. It would be useful for him to think about the work from the practitioner's point of view as well as the client's.

"We work holistically," Hathai said from

where she stood back to avoid interfering. "Some people know it as part of the Indian system of Ayurvedic health, or as traditional Chinese medicine, in which the energy lines in the body become blocked or diseased as opposed to having a healthy flow. It has also to do with acupressure points."

Esme added, "Aroon will move and stretch you in a way that is also known as assisted yoga."

With that, Aroon had Jackson lie face down on the mat on the floor. "Thai massage is done on the floor and with the recipient wearing loose and comfortable clothing. And we use no oils. Very unlike Western massage," Hathai said. Aroon began pressing Jackson's feet with his open palms. And then his legs and arms, which was to awaken his energy.

"It's thought that this type of bodywork might have originated with Buddha's own physician twenty-five hundred years ago, who learned from Indian medicine and integrated it into a regime for good health. The process helps with circulation, mobility, strengthening the immune system, even anxiety and headaches."

As they spoke, Aroon began pulling on Jackson's legs, grasping him with remarkable strength for a man his size. "The giver and the receiver become very connected during the treatment. Jackson, I can see your muscles releasing, perhaps because your body is following Aroon's instincts."

He stretched, then compressed, then rocked each limb, indeed putting Jackson's body into yoga-like positions. And there was more surrender involved when Aroon did walk on Jackson's back, steadying himself by holding on to an apparatus hung from the ceiling for specifically that purpose. Eventually, Aroon ended the session by pulling on Jackson's toes and fingers and ears. It was an unforgettable experience. No wonder it was Esme's favorite type of massage.

For someone who had little regard for massage, he'd undergone a metamorphosis. He hadn't had as much tightness as he had when he'd been to Dr. Singh's office. Although they'd been busy, it had indeed been a much-needed vacation from his usual grind. He suspected it had more to do with Esme's company than anything else. Nonetheless, his respect for these serious disciplines was profound.

"Okay, you sold me. That was incredible."

They decided to go out and enjoy some of Bangkok. Neither knew the city well.

Esme said, "I've never gone to the floating markets."

"Me, either. I know they've become more tourist attraction than anything else but I'd like to go."

Hathai recommended a famous one. Jackson knew that the floating markets used to be the main method by which food and other goods were transported along the country's rivers and canals. Because people settled near them, the culture of riverside shopping was essential to the city's livelihood. Nowadays, shoppers would find fruits and vegetables and a myriad of cooked food and sweets, also clothes, crafts and souvenirs. He quickly arranged for a private boat and driver, and they got to the riverfront and set sail.

"Wow, look at how many boats are on the river."

Indeed, dozens of vessels navigated their way in and around each other. "What do you want to eat? That was my ulterior motive," he said with a wink.

"They say Thailand has the best fruit in the world." She pointed to merchants on the riverbank selling fresh fruit. There was more of the ubiquitous mango, looking as inviting as it had on the platter Hathai served them earlier. Also on display were unusual fruits like mangosteen, with its dark shell and tender white segments inside. Rambutan, with its red spiky rind. The beautiful dragon fruit, white fleshed with black seeds inside surrounded by a vivid purple outer skin. And the famous durian, which was to be a love-it-or-hate-it item because of its extreme smell.

"What do you want to start with?"

"We'll have fruit after. Let's start with something spicy."

"Like you." He didn't necessarily mean to say that but it tripped from his mouth. The sun-kissed highlights of her hair glistened and her lips looked as juicy as the fruits vendors cut and sold in clear bags at the riverbanks. He followed his impromptu comment with an impromptu kiss, something he'd been working on holding back from all day at the spa as he didn't want to make Esme uncomfortable. Among the chatter and commerce of people in the boats and along the banks, conversing, bargaining, yelling out to each other, he kissed her succulent lips again and again, not able to pull away, as if his very life depended on it.

His hands lifted to hold her smooth cheeks, both their faces moist from the natural humidity. He wanted to find a way to join their bodies together, to become not two but one entity, the sum most definitely more potent than its parts. He glued his mouth to hers until they had to break away to catch their breaths and return to a stasis. Jackson noticed the boat driver had his head slightly bowed, which he was sure was in politeness to not watch the two of them kiss and to try to conceal the sweet smile that their display brought to his lips. Even a couple of vendors in boats alongside them giggled in approval.

"So. Spicy. Food, that is."

"I want to try boat noodles," she stated decisively. They saw the boats where pots of noodles were being prepared right on board. Their driver brought them close enough to one of the vendors to make a purchase and they could hardly wait to dig in.

"Oh, my gosh, these are scrumptious," he exclaimed after two bites.

"The broth is so flavorful with both the beef and the pork meats, the dark soy and the chilis."

"I want this every day. We'll have to find a place in New York that makes them well." *We'll* have to. Hmm, he was referring to that as if it was the most obvious thing in the world. *We.* Like they were a typical foodie couple who might travel throughout the New York boroughs in search of new tastes. Was that what was happening? He could no longer imagine a different reality. A New York without Esme. Kissing anyone else on the streets of Stockholm. Of making passionate, rapturous love after the mud bath in Oaxaca. Eating these very noodles on this very boat with someone other than her. Unthinkable.

"Okay, but we have to find somewhere authentic in Queens or somewhere. No fancy-schmancy."

Esme had opened up a door he thought was closed. He felt her in his bones. His priorities had changed. Her. It was her. Sharing boat noodles wasn't supposed to fill his heart. It was noodles, for heaven's sake. But everything with her made him stand up and take heed. He wasn't just pushing through anymore. He was awake and alive. A boat came by and the merchant was selling mango with sticky rice and coconut milk, a most perfect dessert after the strong flavors they'd just eaten. Esme bought a bowl and with her fingers, she fed him a piece of the ripe and luscious fruit. It was the sweetest thing he'd ever tasted.

Esme was sure she was in a dream, or watching a movie. This couldn't be fact. That she was kissing Jackson in a riverboat in Bangkok. Jetting around the world, visiting spas and kissing and now fitting in some tourist pleasures. Pleasures. After fantasizing about it, had she literally picked up a piece of mango and fed it into Jackson's lips? Her fingers tingled from the contact with his mouth, making her want to feed him all the mango in the world and lick the juice that remained on his lips.

He ran the tip of his tongue around his mouth after another bite of fruit. Was that just cruel, forcing her to witness that? Could a person be jealous of a mango? It got to touch his lips and tongue. Well, that was just it, she thought. She had no claim on those powerful lips, a mouth that had made her body shudder for hours. The mango didn't have to ask her permission for his lips. Still, she looked at the glistening orange slices and scowled at them. How dare they?

"Why don't we do an event for the investors when they're in New York for the meeting?" she said quickly, nudging her mind off of lucky mango slices. "We can do it big with some nice food and decorations and give them some mini-treatments. I can do a presentation about benefits and ancient treatments. It'll be great."

"I love how confident you are about this."

"I've been honing this concept for a while. I just didn't think my opportunity was actually coming right now. It's all presenting itself in my mind. I want to focus on women's wellness." She was more used to disappointment, so she didn't get her hopes up about things. Parents in the throes of a fight with each other had tried to bribe her loyalty with promises of a special gift or shopping money. Then once the argument was over and they were back to short-lived bursts of basic decency toward each other, the promises to Esme were forgotten. So she didn't know when her specific scheme for running a spa was going to come to fruition but now she knew it would be someday. Maybe simply saying that good things come to those who wait was real?

"An event is a great plan. The investors love razzle-dazzle."

Wasn't it okay if she gave him another kiss? Yes, she'd vowed to avoid a personal life and the potential hurt it could bring. But that thinking had become ridiculous and limiting. Was it possible that life had made a seismic shift for her? That by spending all of this time with Jackson she could understand just how good it could be to be a *we* under the right circumstances. That what she needed was someone to believe in her, who wouldn't drag her down and take more than they gave. Maybe she needed Jackson. To get her out of her rut and see herself through his eyes and with that, she could conquer the world. Jackson had enriched her life beyond measure, not stolen from it. Maybe *alone* had been a defensive mechanism that she didn't need to hang on to anymore.

She hadn't forgotten that when she was a young child her mother had told her that she'd once wanted to have a career, perhaps go to college. Then she'd met Esme's father and because there was just enough family money to live on, he talked her out of it. They soon had Esme and became nonfunctional, rarely leaving their apartment and teaching Esme to manage their needs as soon as she was old enough. Her mother never took even the smallest step to encourage Esme to pursue the dreams that she herself hadn't.

Could it be that history didn't repeat itself? Couldn't Esme make the jump? Break the mold?

She'd be lying if she didn't admit that spectacular lovemaking was part of the picture. Jackson had coaxed more sensation, awareness and sensitivity than her body had ever known. And she wasn't afraid to be impulsive with him, to do what felt natural and spontaneous, with her own lips, her hands, every part of her. Even though she said they'd satisfied their urge to explore each other and wouldn't do it again, she mentally tossed that rule over the boat and watched it float down the river in between merchants selling pad thai and T-shirts. Yes, she could let him in a little closer. Maybe she'd never devote herself to someone and the risk and obligations that might entail. But she could do this. Have this time with an accomplished and sensual man. She deserved the progress of it. She could keep that separate from long-term worries.

She leaned over and took one of his earlobes between her teeth. The sumptuous dark rumble that came out of him was electrifying. She opened her mouth to let her tongue trace his ear, enjoying that one small move to its fullest. "Jackson," she whispered.

"Yes."

"I have an idea of what I want to do with the rest of this mango." She gestured to the bowl she'd set down on the boat's bench.

"Is that right?"

"Mmm-hmm," she said with a kiss to the private spot behind his ear. "But I'm going to have to show it to you back at the house." Hathai had evening plans and wouldn't return home until late.

CHAPTER TEN

"Do you want to stop?" Jackson asked while taking off Esme's shirt when they got back to the house. They had dropped their belongings and purchases on the table and then crashed into an embrace, grabbing for each other tightly, as if their lives depended on it. Did they?

"No." She appreciated his little verification of her consent, but stopping was not an option. Not while his bites, one after the other, were making a line from her jaw down to where her throat met her shoulders. Her back arched at the sensation. His mouth was both commanding and questioning at the same time, wanting her to tell him more and more. She crooked her neck in the opposite direction to allow him wider access and a moan escaped her vocal cords when he took it. "I definitely don't want to stop."

He continued with his slow, erotic mouth for as long as she wanted him to. She remembered a time with a guy named Rob she'd been with for a few dates. It had actually been the first and one of the only times she'd really experienced sexual pleasure with someone. However, as soon as he noticed her responding to what his hands were doing to her, he pulled away, as if her enjoying it meant she was finished. With Jackson, it was a green light to keep going, and he seemed to relish doing so.

"Esme," he exhaled with a desperate gratification when she unbuttoned his shirt in return. It was equally exciting to know that she was arousing him, also not something she'd ever had validation of before.

And then their motions became like two flowers in bloom, her throat, his shirt buttons, opening, releasing, bending toward each other.

"We said we wouldn't do this again."

"Yup."

"Yup."

They issued their one-syllable protective thought but didn't halt what they were doing even for a second. After the kiss in Stockholm, they'd decided. In Oaxaca they changed that to a one-time license to be intimate. Now here they were, defying that rule, unable to keep away from each other.

How was it that, instead, she felt liberated by Jackson? Perhaps because of all the respect he'd shown her, relying on her professionally, making all that she'd been through to get to this point worthwhile. The quick trip around the world with him was the stuff of fantasy. They'd both had a rebirth and both were still forming, finding their new shapes. That fit into each other. She hadn't even realized how much she needed the affirmation he'd given her.

At the moment, though, after she'd peeled his shirt off his body, her mind was on a quick dash to the table to get the sliced mango they'd bought on the market boat that she'd brazenly promised to continue employing in a private way.

"Oh, yeah, you said there was more about that mango."

She took a piece of the fruit from its bag and held it between her teeth. She approached him and wrapped her arms around his neck to bring him closer. Then she used the piece of mango to draw a line with its juices starting from his Adam's apple and heading downward. The journey was such a turn-on to her, painting him with the mango, marking him, if only for the moment, as hers. She moved slowly down his solid chest, still gripping the fruit with her teeth. When she'd painted that line all the way down to the top of his pants, the task was complete. She coaxed him down into the chair behind him.

"Now what?" His smoldering stare asked the question.

"It seems to be true that Thailand grows the sweetest fruit in the world." She could hardly believe the words coming out of her mouth, so sexual with a courage that she was half faking but somehow believing that if she acted that way it would become so. She leaned over him in the chair using her hands to bolster herself on the armrests so she could hover over him.

"Delicious. Yes," he graveled out, his voice husky and sounding like three in the morning. She brushed her mouth against his but then lowered herself to begin to taste the sweet juice she'd just painted on him. She sunk to the top of his pants and took her first lick there. Indeed, the fruit mixed with the musk that was him was an absolutely intoxicating combination that made her body undulate this way and that, moving to the music his body made her hear. She used the flat of her tongue to work up his torso. A groan forced its way out of him, a sound he didn't seem to have much control over. "Mmm, that feels ridiculously good."

"I want it to." The charge rattled through her again, him acknowledging that what she was doing was favorable to him. The more he gave back to her in that way, the more she wanted to keep doing it. A focused, long, thin lick up his very center made his head roll back, and his lips parted as his even louder groan filled the room. As did the sheer sensuality. The confidence did become real, her body swaying above him, a full-grown woman aware of her wiles. She felt a whole different person inside when she was with him. She didn't understand such magical powers but they were true.

Then as she covered his mouth with hers, she took the thoughts even further. That she was willing to risk for this. For him. That's what it came down to, wasn't it? Risk? She didn't have a crystal ball to look into the future. Maybe embarking on this partnership with Jackson, the personal one and the professional one, would be a total disaster.

Maybe she'd give her all and end up jobless and brokenhearted. At least she would have done something. She'd opened up enough to try. Her heart knew it would be worth it and that if she didn't do it she'd regret it for the rest of her days.

Jackson placed his hands under her arms and pulled them up, kissing them into a lip lock. What was there in life without taking a chance? She, who'd thought it out so carefully, how to avoid being anyone's pawn, evading trust, never planning to relent. She'd grown a hard shell. She thought of it as her protection. But with armor, she wouldn't let things in and she would keep things out. Funny how that had seemed the right thing to do in the past, and now it made no sense at all. It wasn't who she was anymore.

He led them to his guest bed and pulled back the silk coverings. His gaze seared through, almost burning holes in her. But then he changed his expression to a majestic smile. Which said he was present, which might have been saying he needed to take a chance, too.

After they'd showered off the mango and all it entailed, Esme and Jackson were ready to go back out and have an evening before they boarded a flight home to New York the next day. Hathai had recommended a bar where they might want to get a drink.

"It's the famous ex-pat bar," Jackson said as they approached the entrance that was made up of six shutter doors, all open to let in the evening breeze. "The Federal."

"Hathai said it was where the Westerners who live in Bangkok met. Businessmen, volunteers, writers and so on."

"As long as I don't see one more mini-Buddha statue." They'd been bombarded with enough cheesy souvenirs at the floating markets earlier.

They entered and, indeed, they were all Westerners sitting apart from one another. Most of the men were dressed in white shirts and khaki pants as Jackson was, presumably the uniform for the humid weather. There were distinctly more men than women there. All eyes turned to Jackson and Esme when they entered.

"Toronto," one of the men called out to them.

"London," yelled another.

"Perhaps. Too well-heeled for the US West Coast," added another still.

"Or Chicago. But they don't look European." This was obviously a game of Guess the Strangers' Origin being played at their expense.

"Certainly not Aussie," the only man with an outback hat voted in.

"Good evening." Jackson called out, deciding that in good manners they should participate. "What are you basing your guesses on?"

"Nothing whatsoever, mate," said the man who had tagged them as not Australian but his accent suggested that *he* was. "We used to be better at it. We've been in Thailand for too long. The heat has made us stupid." That comment gained a couple of sniggers from around the room.

"We were always stupid, Callum," someone disagreed.

"New York," Jackson answered flatly. One of the men in back began singing about making a brand-new start of it.

"What are you drinking?" asked the bartender, an Asian man who spoke with a British accent.

"Whiskey," Esme called out.

"The lady dabbles in the dark spirits." The man with the Australian accent, Callum, leered at her as he said that. Which ruffled Jackson right away. Was that some sort of flirt? Jackson thought it was rude to comment when a woman walked into a bar with a man. Even more so if she was alone but, nonetheless, he bristled at the unexpected focus on Esme.

He lightly took her elbow, not wanting to seem too possessive, as they made their way in between some empty tables to get to the bar and retrieve their drinks. He sensed this was a pub full of regulars who drank together and were gruff but well intentioned.

"To the Sher." Esme tipped her glass to clink his, seemingly less aware of the vibes in the room than he was.

"To the Sher indeed," he toasted. That she so genuinely cared about the spa moved him.

After they finished their drink, Callum approached Esme, adjusting his hat on his head. Jackson wondered why he wore a hat indoors at all. "Buy you another? Or are you and Mr. New York together? In marital bliss even?" he rasped into Esme's ear, perhaps thinking he was whispering but the volume was well within Jackson's range.

This was getting ridiculous. Was this guy trying to provoke a fight? Maybe that's what drunk ex-pats did when they were bored. The equally boring habit of his jealousy and pessimism crept in. Between the parents that were so icy they'd never even notice the other one's interactions, to the wife that cheated on him with mind, body, soul and wallet, he didn't have much of an example of ethical relationships. He'd made a decision to never need that education, which was how he'd been living for years. Until Esme.

He looked at Callum as if from a distance, in an objective view. Sure, lots of men were going to be attracted to Esme. Why wouldn't they be? She was gorgeous but in a friendly way, wholly approachable. No wonder she was so well suited to the needs of clients. She was also smart and kind. Then he thought of *her* objectively. Even if he was to strip off those bandages that kept his hurt hidden from the sun, was she? After a childhood full of manipulation, she said she'd never take a chance on love. He had no reason to disbelieve her. Well, other than the last few days where they'd been as exposed as they possibly could. Something given openheartedly to each other. Somehow their barricades had been toppled over, despite their best efforts.

Did they want to leave them demolished, or build them up again?

Was it only temporary? Were they going to zip up their coats along with their hearts when they got back to New York? Jackson didn't want to. While Livia had destroyed his hope, Esme brought its promise back. Esme was nothing like his ex-wife. He was sure that if she was ever in any kind of liaison with a man she'd be trustworthy and faithful to him, unless they had agreed otherwise. Without even answering the drunk stranger Callum's question as to whether Esme was together with Jackson, he said to her, "Let's go get dinner. Night, all." He laid some money down on the bar. Most of the men growled indifferently.

Jackson ushered them out because he surely didn't want to spend their last night in Thailand, their last night on this globe-trot, dealing with this Callum fellow or his own overreaction. While they'd been inside, it had started to rain. As they walked, he kept checking the expression on her face to see if she was appreciating the walk as much as he was. "Do you want to keep walking in the rain or should we seek cover?"

"I love it. It's refreshing. It's almost sticky on your skin." He wanted to touch her arm, or kiss it even, but they were walking.

"I hope I wasn't wrong in my assumption that you weren't interested in that man's attention?"

"No, but I'm not sure that was a battle I needed fought for me." Obviously, Esme was a very strong person. If she ever was to be with someone, she'd never be the little woman being overpowered by the big possessive male. Her fierce self-sufficiency, born of necessity, was something that was so compelling about her.

"Well, he bothered *me* so I wanted to get away before I provoked him."

In addition to learning about all of the amazing techniques and skills involved in the healing arts of spa, he'd never spent this much time with a woman. Full stop.

"What happens when we get back to New York?" He blurted what he only intended to answer in his mind.

"We put together a quick investor event. I've been texting and emailing with Trevor, and he's already got an event manager and caterer on call."

"I meant us."

"Are *we* an *us*?" They both chuckled at the pronouns.

He reached for her hand to hold as they turned a street corner and said hard things. He needed her palm in his to center himself. Motor scooters, bicycles and cars all fought for territory in the busy evening. "This time with you has completely caught me by surprise. I've told you all the things I had firmly believed were not for me."

"And now?"

He shrugged. "Now, it's a new dawn. This trip made it different. You made it different."

She focused her eyes forward; she needed a minute. He felt unwrapped, even though he hadn't made any declarations. In fact, his thoughts were a jumble as she asked the very thing he didn't know the answer to. "What does happen now?"

"Is that entirely my decision?" His answer was a bit short and he chided himself after he'd said it. But he was confused about what he should dream of. And what would never be.

"Fair point."

It seemed like neither of them were saying what had to be said. What did he really want? "I never imagined that I would care about someone the way I've come to care about you." He saw a flicker in her eyes. "I see now that I'm cutting myself off from too much if I keep myself closed and locked. Which would all just be a bunch of theoretical musings if I hadn't met you. You've changed everything for me. Now I want to explore my heart. I can't see going back to New York to a work-only situation."

"Meeting you has shaken all the pillars that I held to be true, too. Nobody has ever made me feel so valued. That's a bigger deal than I'd ever thought it was. I assumed I'd be my only cheerleader."

And then he kissed her. In the rain. Their clothes soaking wet and clinging to their bodies. It had only been a few nights since Stockholm but it felt like a lifetime. He and Esme under the sun or the moon or the snow or the stars. Together.

CHAPTER ELEVEN

THERE WERE A million things to do as soon as Jackson and Esme got back to New York. It was good to be busy because everything that happened on the trip had her walking on unsteady ground. The Sher and her managerial duties, and planning the investor event, would keep her mind occupied. Elation propelled her every step but she still wasn't sure what was going to be with Jackson. During the plane ride home they'd committed to a sort of a let's-see policy as neither knew whether they could truly open themselves to the other in the long term.

They'd arrived in the evening and paid a quick visit to the closed spa just to make sure everything was okay. Which, naturally, it was in Trevor's capable hands. Once they turned off all of the lights, set the alarm and went out the door, Jackson voiced a dilemma.

"You know I don't actually keep an apartment in New York. Can I book us a hotel suite or…?" His voice trailed off, not sure how to finish, obviously inviting her to. They hadn't talked about the nuts and bolts of that we'll-see arrangement. Was he going to stay with her? As in day and night, work and… not work?

Instead of overthinking it, she was decisive. Terrified, but putting one foot in front of the next. "Why don't you stay with me? My place is tiny but we're going to be spending a lot of time at the spa."

The most charming grin came across his face, as if she'd given him a gift he'd really wanted. "I would love that." On the little landing outside the spa door, under the safety light that cast a wide glow across their faces, he reached over and wound her scarf around her neck.

"Here we are." The driver dropped them off at the curb in front of her apartment building and they took the staircase to the second floor. "I'm sure it's the size of some people's closet."

"I don't have a home so yours is, by definition, bigger than mine," he said as she opened her front door. He glanced around, at what she thought were tasteful, budget-friendly furnishings. On the wall she had hung two poster-sized photographs, one of rain falling in a forest and another of sunset over a beach. A small smile crossed his lips.

"What?"

"Nothing. These are just so you." He pointed to the posters. "Something to meditate on right up on your walls."

"Don't knock it until you've tried it," she mock-snipped.

They kissed softly and quietly. She rarely had anyone in her apartment, most certainly not a man. She thought his energy might feel oppressive but it was like he belonged. His essence filled the apartment, a kind of fragrance she could never get enough of. Was he a tree that could grow roots? Would he be able to stop chasing himself and settle into her? Would she, him?

She said as she shook her scattered head, "I'm whacked out again from the time change. How about I order a pizza and we can make some quick notes about what we need to do in the next few days so we can get right to it in the morning?"

"Sounds like a good idea."

After they ate and, in fact, outlined an action plan, she went into the small bedroom to put fresh sheets on the bed and lay out some clean towels for Jackson to use. By the time they collapsed into bed, it was the wee hours. Esme was unused to sleeping on one side of the bed rather than in the middle. At first it bothered her and her body tensed. It didn't need to be said that they wouldn't do anything other than sleep tonight, as they were exhausted. But while Jackson fell right to sleep, she kept her eyes glued to the ceiling for as long as she could stand it, and then rolled over to admire him. His gorgeous face was a work of art she could stare at endlessly, the way his features were so perfectly arranged. The long eyelashes, the elegantly sloped nose, the plump lips.

Was she going to play house with this man, and was it really playing after all? If so, it was a dangerous game. If she lost, she could lose big. If Jackson was to further break what was already broken, she didn't know if she'd be able to put herself back together. That's why she'd vowed never to let someone this close. And yet every fiber in her being told her that this would be worth it. *He* was worth it.

Although her musings kept her up most of the night, they had to hit the ground running if they were going to pull off this event before the investors voted on whether to stay involved in the Sher. Prior to their arrival, Esme had asked Trevor to rearrange her office and put a computer and desk in for Jackson so they could work.

"Will this do?" Trevor asked when they came in.

"Perfect, thanks. How are the twins?"

"Exhausting. Every second of it precious." He showed her a photo on his phone of the babies and Omari, whose smile said it all.

Esme and Jackson settled themselves in and began ironing out the details. The board president of the investors group was to come by in a couple of hours so they wanted to give him a mini-presentation of what they were planning.

"We're doing the cacao theme. Like in Oaxaca, everyone likes those tastes and aromas, and it has medicinal value. I can weave it into the food and use it in the treatments. I can even get some scented lotions and lip balms so we can do a gift bag they can take home."

A smile spread across his face. "In a million years I wouldn't have thought of something like that."

"I guess you're pretty lucky to have me around," she joked. She wasn't really joking but she voiced it with a laugh so that she wouldn't sound arrogant.

"In more ways than one," he replied in a flat voice that slid down her sternum. Although, there wasn't time for her to melt into goo.

"Continuing with the theme, of course we'll do a mole with lunch. Tamales would be good but they require a fork and sitting down. Let me think of something easier. I'll text Luis at Bajo el Sol. He'll have some ideas for me." Her mind filled with their time in Oaxaca, the *sobada* protocol, the mud therapy after which they made love for the first time. What a magical place that was. She wondered if Bajo el Sol would always be a touchstone place for her, the smell of the mountains, the almost supernatural treatments. It was perhaps the most unique spa she'd ever been to. She looked forward to the next time she could visit.

"Luis and Cozumel." Jackson smiled to himself, perhaps having a nice memory of his own.

"And we'll do a *tejate*."

"What's that?"

"It's a drink made from cacao and maize. It's high in antioxidants and tastes really rich. And we'll finish with a bittersweet brownie made with coffee and cinnamon or something like that to end on a heavily chocolate note."

"I have to concentrate on the financial prospectus I had my accountant put together. If you don't stop talking about chocolate, we may not have a spa soon."

Trevor's voice came through the intercom, "Brent Lloyd is here."

"Have you met the board president, Brent?" Jackson looked up from his computer screen to ask Esme.

"No, would I have had any reason to?" After all, she was previously only the spa's manager, responsible for things like schedules and supplies. She wasn't involved with investors or long-term planning decisions. Until now. She took a breath so long it started down in her toes and ended above her head. She was at the big table now.

"I'm just printing something. I'll be there in a minute."

"Hello, I'm Esme Russo, the spa director," she said as she approached Brent Lloyd in the reception area. Wow, that was the first time she'd identified herself out loud as director. The sound of it gave her a thrill. Proof that hard work and perseverance paid off. She was an unlikely success story. Who couldn't wait to pay it forward, to give someone else the break they needed to grasp their goals. She intended to start with Trevor. And then maybe her own children someday? Hers and Jackson's?

As to Brent Lloyd, did she perceive the tiniest wince on his face when he shifted his weight from one hip to the other? He was a salt-and-pepper-haired man, nice looking with aging skin, wearing a fine leather jacket atop his dress pants.

"Brent, if you don't mind me asking, are you in pain?" His body language all but announced that something wasn't right. She always pointed out observations like that and would continue to whether to prince or pauper or board president.

"How did you know?" he asked in surprise.

"I can see it in your stance."

"Can you? I have lower back pain. It's been worse lately."

"Do you spend a lot of time on a computer?"

"Yeah, hours upon hours. Seven days a week."

"Is it a stabbing pain or a dull ache?"

"Ache."

"I may be able to relieve the pressure a bit. Do you want me to give it a try?"

He rubbed his lower back, which caused him enough discomfort that his jaw clenched. "Sure. Anything would help."

She invited him to take his jacket off and sat him down in one of the chairs. She began some long strokes the heel of her palm to his lower back, the lumbar section, then used the tips of her thumbs to add more pressure.

"Tell me if I'm creating pain because that's the last thing we want to do." She pressed in but kept it gentle and could feel each small area she worked on loosen up. "There we go. Do you do physical therapy or get massages?"

"I used to. Then once I get busy, things like that just fall by the wayside."

She concentrated on a particularly tensed-up spot.

"Thank you, I can feel the difference already."

"So can I talk you into booking some treatments at somewhere convenient for you?"

"I live upstate but I'll have my wife make some appointments for me. I don't know why I stopped doing the thing that was helping." He let out a chuckle and she joined him.

"We all think we're too busy. Believe me, I hear that from a lot of people. Do you do any stretching?"

"Another thing I've let lag."

"Or applying heat or ice, or both?"

"Now you're making me look bad."

She smiled and glanced up from Brent to see Jackson standing in the office doorway as if frozen. His eyes bore into her but not in the sensual way they had been for the past couple of days. No, his look was equal parts fury and shock.

"Jackson, what's wrong?"

After a long day's work, Jackson and Esme decided to go for a walk. They ambled without talking through Tribeca up to Greenwich Village, passing shops, restaurants, galleries and all Manhattan had to offer. Jackson was agitated, not from the excitement of the city but because he hadn't gotten over what he witnessed earlier at the spa.

"Are you going to tell me what's bothering you so much?" Obviously, his mood was palpable.

"It's madness."

"So, it's madness. If it's real to you, it matters."

He loved that she said that but was he going to tell her things that he considered shameful? If he was ever going to change and be able to commit to her, he'd have to. And he wanted to. He did want to.

"You've been off the whole afternoon."

Did anything escape this woman? It didn't seem so! "When Brent Lloyd came in and you were touching him, I felt that jealousy I can't seem to control. Which I know is destructive."

"Are you kidding me, Jackson?" He could hear the annoyance in her voice. "I could see he was having some pain. I offered to help him out."

"That's what I assumed." His face became hot. He was embarrassed. His ire had risen in Bangkok with the pushy Australian man at that pub. He'd even had a twinge in Stockholm when he felt that massage therapist Anders's eyes had lingered on Esme for too long. "Brent is a good guy, president of the board, I've known him for years. But when I saw the two of you…my mind just spiraled back to… I know it makes no sense."

"To what, specifically?"

"To my ex-wife. Not only that she had cheated on me both in business and with other men. The whole idea of trust. When I saw you with Brent it was like you had been deceiving me or doing something behind my back."

"Because I was touching a man in a professional capacity?"

"I told you. My suspiciousness is sometimes so fierce it feels like it could eat me alive."

He could tell by the set of her face that she was troubled, maybe even angry. This was really his moment of reckoning. The time had come. He knew he'd stay alone and bitter unless he broke free of the past. They walked at least three blocks again without a word.

Esme broke the silence with, "After my parents used me in their war games, I'm not playing anymore."

"You shouldn't have to."

Washington Square Park came into view, with its famous arch. NYU students gathered in pairs and groups, exuberantly talking and gesturing. Others sat alone, studying or typing furiously into their phones. People walked dogs. Older men played chess. Tourists posed for photos with the arch in the background. Jackson wanted to be part of this pulsing New York. To make a life in a truly great city with this magnificent woman. Could he possibly get out of his own way?

"Jackson," she began and turned her head to look at his face while they walked, "I want to move forward with my life. Going on the trip with you, our arrangement about me becoming spa director, the positivity heading me in the right direction. There's something I haven't told you."

"What's that?"

"I didn't need to stay at the Sher for four years before applying for directorships. After a year or two and all of my previous experience, I'd learned enough and I had the right ideas."

"Why did you stay?"

"Because while I project myself as confident, I got lost in doubt. I let myself loll.

I was tired after thirty-two years of serving others. Even though I wanted to, I didn't really know if I could go further."

"What changed your mind?"

"I needed my confidence boosted. The old days were pulling me back down again. You gave me what I needed."

"Which you deserve."

"That's right, I do. If you care about me, don't hold me back, or let me hold myself back."

"That's the last thing I want to do." He had to do better. He owed it to Esme. He owed it to himself.

A group of young women rushed by, a cloud of squeals and perfume and colorful beanies.

"I'm willing to go further with you than I ever imagined I would with anyone," she said. "But I'm still fragile, and I always will be. I could shatter if injured. So if you can't do this, decide that now. Don't make me put myself in so much danger."

"Of course, I want to. I wish it was as simple as that. Just to have courage and faith."

"You want to start from a place of total *distrust*?"

They both laughed. "Because it's only up

from there. Be patient with me." Two dogs barked at each other in greeting. Jackson gave Esme a kiss on her forehead. Horns honked and people walked by. He teased her with an overly dramatic raise of one eyebrow. "What, so you like that Brent Lloyd?"

She pretended to slap his shoulder. "Yeah, I gotta go. I have dinner plans with him."

"You rascal," he said as he pulled her in for a hug. "Seriously, what do you want to do for dinner?"

"Spend it with you being threatened by every move I make."

"That's a great idea. No wonder I named you spa director."

They walked the perimeter of Washington Square Park like tourists, pointing out buildings and trees. Students holding hands while lugging backpacks heavy enough to topple them. Two older men arm in arm as they slowly strolled. A pregnant woman walking alongside a man pushing a stroller with a sleeping toddler in it. Love was in the air in New York. Maybe it had always been, maybe not just in New York but everywhere. She just never thought it would apply to her.

"What do you feel like eating?" he asked as they ambled.

Even that, even him asking a simple question, made the world different. Growing up, she was never asked what she wanted to eat. She was lucky if her parents gave her enough money to get groceries for the three of them, always sending her with a shopping list to adhere to.

"Weren't we going to try to find good boat noodles here, like the ones we had at the floating market in Thailand?"

"Ooh, that sounds great. Let me look it up." He pulled his phone out of his pocket and began swiping a search.

It wasn't going to be an easy task, creating something solid and long-lasting with him. The business with Brent Lloyd earlier was almost more than she could handle. Jackson could see himself in action and explain his rationale yet he couldn't stop those old feelings from resurfacing. He felt some kind of certainty that she'd betray him in some way, trick him, further tarnish his dead parents' disappointment. She couldn't make his problems hers. Although, perhaps that was what a true partnership was, helping to hold each other's monsters.

If she let herself go down a certain path of thinking, it was actually touching that she arose jealousy in him. It was because he wanted her only to himself. Albeit unhealthy and unworkable, it was a measure of devotion. She'd surely never been protected before, which she had to admit was welcome in that bar in Bangkok with that aggressive Australian man. Maybe they could reframe Jackson's behavior into something positive while he hopefully *grew out of it* as time went on and he saw her as loyal. Or maybe that was asking too much of herself. Yet she knew she'd regret it for the rest of her life if she didn't try.

"I've got a couple of places in Queens." He showed her his phone. "Let's try this one tonight and we'll compare it with these others until we find the best one. I'll call a car."

They slid into the small wooden booth in the window of the restaurant. The smells alone were making her hungry. They ordered two different flavors of boat noodles. The server, who was also the owner, nodded approvingly at their ability to dig into the spicy cauldrons of noodles and broth without a flinch. They also ordered Isan chicken.

"We'll take the rest home and have it for lunch."

"What makes you think there will be leftovers?" He smiled and dug into a piece of chicken marinated and coated in spices, grilled to charred perfection.

They sat and shot the breeze, as the saying went. After all that hard stuff with Brent Lloyd earlier, they needed the casual quiet of a window seat and some comforting food in a low-key neighborhood. He'd been right that while their ravenous hunger was satiated, they still managed to pick at the savory chicken until there was none left to take home.

Home. Did he live with her now? It was only their second night back in New York but there had been no further talk of him going to a hotel. Nor did she want there to be. She wanted him wrapped around her. All night long. When they got *home* she washed her face and brushed her teeth. While he was in the bathroom, she turned down the bedsheets and put on some soft music. When he stepped out, she was there to greet him, standing on tiptoe to wrap her arms around his neck. They were finally relaxed, warm, with full bellies and a good workday behind them. She led him to the bed and guided him down. *He* was her new home.

If she could go the distance. As she lay in bed practicing her deep breathing before going to sleep, she made some decisions on her boundaries.

CHAPTER TWELVE

"I WAS GOING to put these out on the front tables," Trevor said as he put the finishing touches on the gift bags for the investor event. "But I think it's too easy for people to forget. I'm having someone taking and returning coats at the door. We could give one to each person when they're leaving."

Esme approved. "Good thinking."

Jackson stepped away from the tech setup he was working on with his marketing people. He came up behind Esme and wrapped his arms around her. "You okay?" he asked. She leaned back into him, knowing she had time for about a twenty-second hug and that was all.

"Yeah." She turned her head back toward him. "You?"

"Ready."

"Go." Lovey time was up. In fact, the first guest arrived, an older woman with white-blond hair.

"Yes, that's a longtime investor." He turned to her. "Millie Abernathy, please meet the spa director and visionary for what we want to do with the Sher, Esme Russo."

Millie's handshake was bony but firm. The woman moved on as someone else came through the door, another woman, this one probably in her forties, with dark hair and skin lacquered with a little too much makeup, in Esme's opinion.

Jackson made introductions. "This is Pia Bravo."

Before Esme could blink, a lively din filled the spa. Guests were served *tejate*, the famous old drink from Oaxaca that had been a refreshment for centuries. People who knew each other reunited while others met for the first time. Out of the corner of her eye she saw Brent Lloyd come in, the man with the lumbar issue that turned out to be a trigger for Jackson. Esme would try her best not to provoke Jackson, but after mulling it over, she wasn't going to be babysitting, or condoning, his behavior. That could only lead to resentment in the end.

"And that's why we invited you to join us today so we can give you a sense of how we see the Sher moving into a highly specialized place of healing that we hope will be cherished by New Yorkers and visitors alike for decades to come," Jackson spoke to the crowd.

Next it was Esme's turn. "Let's gather together and get centered with a simple breathing technique to ground us. Breathe in slowly through your nose," she said to the attentive audience, "and slowly out through your mouth. Concentrate on making it smooth and seamless. In. And out. Today I'm going to explain a bit about the Mayan traditions of *sobada* that we want to become foremost practitioners of." She gave her multimedia presentation, finishing with, "What we're going to do now is give everyone who would like a mini-treatment to get a hands-on sense of what we're doing."

The freelance massage therapists Esme had brought in who knew how to do the Mexican Mayan massages fanned out in the room and invited the investors into treatment rooms and a few makeshift areas they'd created in the common spaces. Of course, it would take years before a therapist could become an expert on a certain technique. This was merely a quick way to introduce the intention and spirit, plus the luxury of the rich and high-quality products used. She'd taught the staff to do a closing ceremony with each person, to wrap them in a makeshift rebozo shawl that they were able to approximate with some scarves Trevor picked up in East Harlem, an area called Little Mexico that had a large population of Mexican residents. They also concluded with a cup of raw cacao, which was thought to have highly medicinal properties.

As she surveyed the event, board president, Brent Lloyd, caught her eye and beckoned her over.

"I want to thank you for your therapeutic touch last time I was here."

"How's your lower back?"

"I wish I could say it was consistently better but it's not with my overuse."

"Can I have a feel?"

"Would you? I'd so appreciate it." She let her hands roam over Brent's lumbar area and inform her of his condition today. Indeed, his muscles were seized up, his body like stone.

"If you could even get one of those hot

and cold packs from a local pharmacy, that might help."

He nodded.

Then, she felt it even before she looked up. From in between people mulling about, she sensed Jackson's eyes piercing into her. A lump in her stomach grew so big it almost burst. Because after all of their talk about recognizing negative patterns, where they came from and the relevance they did and didn't have, none of it amounted to anything when actions spoke louder than words.

The look she returned to him was one of anguish. Had all they'd said to each other just been drivel? She should have known that, in the end, they were like children playing dress-up. Despite them sincerely wanting to, the clothes didn't fit. She knew in an instant that they would both lose the match.

"Esme, is something the matter?" Brent noticed that her hands had gone slack, had stopped concentrating on his muscle pain. Jackson's face, contorted, threw daggers at her. The realization sent devastation coursing through her. But she had to keep herself together, with as much will as that took. That's what professionals did.

Yet she couldn't. All she could do was

stare back at Jackson while he glared at her through arms holding colorful Mexican shawls. Perhaps both of them coming to the same conclusion. That nothing could work between them if she wasn't free to be herself. She'd thought maybe she cared enough about him to accept him, damage and all. Maybe someone who had herself come from a firmer base could have done it. In the end, though, she was too weak for him.

There was only so much she could do for him while still respecting the promises she'd made to herself. Which let anger slowly bubble up in her body. Because she'd thought they'd found a way to each other. But those seething glares of his were too much, not in their menace but in their sadness, both hurtful and hurt. Her anger quickly blended with sorrow. The notion that she could see his emotional issues clinically, and therefore not have them affect her this much, vanished. She was only human. He drained her. It could only get worse.

"Excuse me," she said to Brent as she stepped away, finding a quiet alcove down the corridor. There, one lone tear dripped out of her eye, which she quickly brushed away with the back of her hand. Two more fell from the other eye. She grabbed a tissue and mopped those with the same vigor, making sure none of the investors could see her.

Jackson knew in his gut. He couldn't put himself or anyone else through this again. Despite how much he wanted to, he couldn't pull himself out of his own wreckage. He'd vowed to never risk again and apparently, he was right to do so. As he'd stood watching Esme talk to Brent Lloyd, the same old thoughts took him over, a speeding train with him tied down on the tracks.

He supposed he'd made some progress. He knew enough not to think there was something untoward going on between Esme and Brent. Although that was only when he could force his rational mind to take the forefront. Because the child's mind, and the young husband's mind, remembered every shard of heartbreak and guilt as if it freshly cracked in him today. If it happened once, it could happen again. Esme would never be able to trust him to trust her. So there was nothing to fight for. It was about more than other men's attention. Their future would be him waiting for her to deceive him as Livia had. She could never tolerate that. Nor should she have to.

His ears rang loud and clear to him the simple message that he was alone in the world and that's how he would remain. He was too volatile. He carried too much baggage.

He'd seen Esme slip down the corridor and he moved to find her. A passerby would just assume they were conversing about spa matters.

"I'm sorry," he said as the truth gushed through him like boiling blood through his veins. "I can't do this. I thought I could but I can't."

"I see."

Those sweet green eyes of hers hooded. He wouldn't subject her to him. To deny himself was better than to squelch her. That's how much she meant to him. She didn't need him, suspicious and prying, keeping tabs and not letting her fly free. No one needed that in their life, but especially not Esme, who'd already borne the brunt of other people's misconduct.

He'd let her think it was simple jealousy. That was easier for both of them. Neither having to face that those demons were a disease, a terminal illness. Never again make a bad decision that would let his parents' memory down. Never be taken on an emotional roller coaster where he'd end up feeling used. He wouldn't survive it again. He'd take the safer route. He might have been able to trust her with the spa. But not with his heart.

"It's better for you. And what's best for you is what matters the most to me now."

CHAPTER THIRTEEN

WHILE SOOTHING THE arthritic left hand of Mrs. Abernathy, Esme was determined not to lose her cool. As she worked the woman's joints, she gazed across the room and observed Jackson standing in a little conversational huddle with three other guests.

"Reducing inflammation can have a big impact," she said, her voice airy, not even sounding like herself.

"It feels better." The older woman's voice floated away.

Jackson looked wound up like a rubber band. His shoulders were up to his ears as they were when he'd first come to visit the spa a few weeks ago. She didn't wish him harm but if he'd just said to her in the corridor what he did and he wasn't affected by it, she'd be even more destroyed. If that was actually possible.

Yet he waved her over. She finished with Mrs. Abernathy's hand and joined him at his circle.

"Esme plans to also incorporate some ancient Eastern medicine techniques into our offerings," he told the group, gesturing for her to turn on the spa talk.

"Energy work has been practiced in the Eastern traditions for centuries and can be so powerful for overall health and wellness," she explained for probably the tenth time today. That voice that didn't seem to even belong to her came out as if she was in a trance.

Really, she was holding back the ocean of tears that wanted to burst forth from her eyes, drenching the room, drenching the building, maybe drenching all of New York. The words coming out of Jackson's mouth spoke to the investors of the Spa at the Sher's future. Esme was no longer certain if those plans still included her. Would she even want them to?

"We like what we see so far," one of the investors told Jackson.

Her zombie voice said to someone, "Thank you for coming."

"I'm so sorry," Jackson whispered in her ear as they ushered out the last of the guests.

Was he apologizing for what he'd said to her in the corridor or that he wasn't able to control himself for saying it during the event? She supposed his knee-jerk reaction to seeing her with Brent Lloyd again got the best of him and he lost his decorum. "Believe me, I came to the same conclusion when you again glared at me like I'd committed a crime. Because I tried to help Brent with his lumbar issue. Your board president, who is a nice man and who it might be beneficial to impress with the work we do here. You're right, Jackson, I can't go on like this."

"I know it seems twisted that not wanting to subject you to me is an act of devotion on my part."

"So you keep saying. Are you congratulating yourself?" All of it was riling her up and now that the guests were gone, she saw no reason to hold back. "Have you ever heard that expression about cutting your nose off to spite your face?"

"Esme." He reached for her hand. She pulled it away. "Esme."

"You're just going to be tortured for the rest of your life? You're so concerned with history repeating itself that you're going to bury what could have been a rebirth. Take the less risky road even though it might not be the one that could give you joy and fulfilment. And end up alone and with health conditions, just like how you started."

"I thought I could do it. I can't."

What would she do now? She wanted the spa directorship. And she'd known this was a possibility, that things wouldn't work out with him personally and that it could cost her the job. In fact, after all of this, could she work with him? Could he work with her? Either way, she'd forever live inside a shell of rumination, of what might have been with him. That she opened her heart once and it was swiftly trampled on. This shift was monumental. The world was suddenly a darker place, a lonely terrain. "You made me rethink everything, Jackson. I will forever regret that I wasn't able to do the same for you."

"No, it's not you. You are the finest person I've ever met."

"I know," she snapped.

"It's my albatross that I'll have to continue to live with."

"If that's what you choose."

The conversation was going around in circles. She absentmindedly began throwing out drinks and food that had been left behind. She wanted to go home. Jackson could book a room at the best hotel in the city. She needed to remove herself from this situation. While she had her hands full of plates, she felt her phone vibrate in her pocket. Once she put her armload down, she pulled it out to see the call she'd missed. It was Cozumel in Oaxaca, her familiar voice saying, "Esme, give me a call as soon as you have a chance. I have a question for you."

Jackson tapped his key card to open the heavy steel door of yet another hotel suite, as he'd done hundreds of times, one door indistinguishable from the next. Just a five-block walk ago, he'd locked up at the Sher and stopped to appreciate the dedication plaque on the door.

In memory of Beatrice and Wesley Finn

Today had been the launch of the newly revamped spa. All of the publicity his staff worked so hard on had paid off. Trevor kept everything running smoothly. It should have been a terrific day. The *New York Times* and the *Village Voice* came, as well as the spa industry trade publications. It was the signal of a new phase for Jackson. Although there was a gaping hole in the proceedings, one about five and a half feet tall with golden highlights in her hair.

He kicked off his shoes and moved to the thirty-fifth-floor window to look out at the city lights. What could have been one of the most transformative days of his life was dampened by the missing component. The piece that was the only thing that could complete him morning, noon or midnight, special days and ordinary ones, too. Instead, this day would have a different history. Of all that wasn't.

Good luck. Those were the last words she'd said to him. After he'd broken up with her, to use a common parlance. It occurred to him for the first time how powerful the word *broke* was. Because he indeed felt broken without Esme. Broken into shards, in fact. Too many to even count. Too numerous to ever put back together as one. *Broken up.*

Good luck. He was going to need it. Luck, or something. To survive losing her. She, who'd made him want to try again. She, who'd reminded him of what he was searching for all those years ago when he mistakenly found Livia. Esme seemed like she could fill the hole inside of him that was desperate for demonstrative love and excitement and passion. Someone to gush over. He thought he was in big, fireworks, trombone-salute love. One that energized him inside and made life worth living.

Good luck. That was three weeks ago. The investors had approved the launch. Esme had worked remotely with Trevor tirelessly helping get everything in order. They named Trevor as spa manager, which was a promotion Esme wanted for him all along. And Jackson returned to hotel life. Room service food that was never quite warm enough. Uniformed housekeepers tracking his packages of laundry.

Oh, how he missed the coziness of Esme's little apartment where he felt like a man at the start of his adulthood whose life was unfolding a little bit at a time. He missed Esme's mismatched coffee mugs. The one shaped like an apple, symbol of the city, had become his favorite. He missed her towels, always fresh and stacked high in the bathroom cupboard, encouraging an indulgent shower. Mostly, he missed being around her.

She'd become his touchstone, his talisman, his password into the world. Nonetheless, despite her physical absence, the reopening came together. She'd been away from him for twenty-one days, each of which he counted with a check mark on his calendar. That was a lie because he really counted the time away from her by the hours. No, the minute. The second, if that was possible.

"Cozumel called me," Esme had explained to him over the phone the day after the investors event. "Remember she was telling us that their spa director, Itza, was going to take maternity time off and that she wasn't sure she'd return. She let Cozumel and Luis know that she wanted substantial time with her family and that they should look for a replacement."

"And of course, they thought of you."

"Yeah, I mean, we've always had a great working relationship."

"When we were there, Cozumel complimented your work with that woman who was having trouble with fertility. She said she'd love to have you back. Why wouldn't she?"

"By the way, the woman, Payaan, did get pregnant."

"That's beautiful." For some reason, a

lump formed in his throat thinking about pregnancy and the desire for family. The continuum of life. What an amazing place Cozumel and Luis had created.

"They want you back. You are both a consummate professional and a true healer."

"It'll give me a start at that directorship I've always wanted. Luis plans to expand, open a second location. It's a great opportunity for me."

He knew her well enough to know that she wasn't saying everything she was thinking. "That's great." His lack of sincerity was audible.

"I'm doing us both a favor." She stopped. It sounded like she was slowing herself down, choosing difficult words. "We couldn't make something personal work. Why have the torture of running a business together? Let's cut each other loose, take the gains with the losses and walk away."

Why did she have to be so smart and logical? On the other hand, if she was swept with emotion and begging for them to keep trying, what would he do? No matter. Of course, she wasn't going to do that even if that was her impulse, after she'd been thoroughly rejected. She wasn't going to sign up for more.

"You'll find someone chomping at the bit to lead the Sher," she continued. "And Trevor is a gem. We did a great thing, you and I. We gave your parents' spa a direction forward."

"No, you did that. I bankrolled a quick trip around the world." Maybe she didn't realize that she'd also brought a dead man back to life. Changed his mental outlook in ways that would inform the rest of his life. *We gave the spa a direction forward*, he silently repeated the words into the recirculated air of the hotel room.

If he loved her, he'd let her go cleanly and completely. Wait. *L.O.V.E.* A word that might have been casually tossed around when he was with Livia but it wasn't until he'd met Esme that he began to even have a cursory understanding of its meaning. Yet he wasn't able to do what love demanded, to be fearless with no promises. It showed someone what was possible. If they believed in the best, giving what they took. He loved Esme. He was in love with her. Which was why she was telling him she was leaving and he was wishing her well. It was the greatest wish he'd ever have. For her to be well. In every way. Thousands of miles in another country or five blocks away. Self-love in action. She was taking care of herself, finally. She had to go, to fly with steel wings and make sure no one ever rusted her again.

"Good luck to you, too," his gravelly voice had creaked out.

He stared at himself in a mirror on the wall for a long while. Indeed, his shoulders were up as high as his ears. He didn't want to die. He inhaled deeply through his nose and exhaled slowly through his mouth as Esme had taught him to.

Finally, he picked up his phone and returned to the website he had been lurking at for a couple of weeks now. A recommendation he'd gotten from Dr. Singh.

On the home page was a photo of tall trees and dirt trails. The graphic read, "Kendrick Washington, Psychologist. Is your past holding you back from what you want?"

CHAPTER FOURTEEN

THE MOON WAS so bright it provided light to what Esme knew were the wee hours. She didn't have her phone with her so didn't know the correct time. After tossing and turning in bed she'd stepped out of the casita and breathed in the cool air of night. She lay down on one of the lounge chairs by the firepit where just a few weeks ago she and Jackson had slowly sipped a mezcal in the mild evening. There were no sounds to be heard at this hour, just a maddening quiet that made her ask the moon a question. How would she clean off her wounds and move on yet again?

She'd spent most of her life fixing things. Placating her parents and compensating for their shortcomings. What would have become of her if she hadn't found her way to that local spa and all those towels to wash? Would she have ended up taking care of a man, repeating her childhood role? Or stuck at a job where she'd never found a passion or calling. Or, for that matter, she could have ended up homeless and destitute. Taking stock under the Mexican sky, it seemed, though, that she had let a man throw her off her balance. In spite of her better instincts.

Earlier this evening, she'd talked to Trevor, who said the opening was a big hit although some of the guests wanted to know where the director with the good breathing techniques was. That made Esme smile, although with a double edge. Maybe she should have been strong enough to stay in New York and run the spa with Jackson, driven enough to put the romantic past behind them. The minute he pushed her away because his own scars hurt too much, she turned her back on him. She didn't stay to fight for the man she'd fallen in love with. The one who she'd never thought she'd meet.

Cozumel gave her a once-over when she came into the kitchen after falling asleep on the lounger. Luis was stirring pots on the stove and looked over. She said, "My, Esme, you don't look happy."

"I'll be okay," Esme said. "I won't let you down."

"I know that. It's you I'm concerned about."

How grateful she was that Cozumel and Luis had become friends, not just colleagues. She'd called Esme three weeks ago, on the day that happened to be the investors event, one of the best and worst days of her life. Taking over the Sher, and she and Jackson together in a way that really felt *together*. A dream she'd never dared before. Until he woke up and turned it into a nightmare.

"Does that handsome Jackson have something to do with it?" Luis asked while putting a mug of *café con leche* in front of Esme. "He was more than just your boss, am I right?"

Esme took a sip of Luis's creamy brew. "I thought he was. It turns out we're not a match."

"No," Cozumel jumped in, "I could feel it in my bones. And see it in the way you looked at each other. You are each other's safe haven." Cozumel's words entered Esme's ears and she kept hearing them over and over in her head. *Haven.* She and Jackson were each other's haven. That was the truth. He wouldn't allow it, though, couldn't let her eyes guide him home no matter how hard she tried.

Had she tried hard enough? He knew what was imprisoning him. That self-awareness itself held promise. With her love, could he break free?

"I made a mistake in falling for someone in the first place. My first real relationship and I managed to choose the wrong person."

"You didn't choose him any more than he chose you." Cozumel shook her head. "Your destinies found you. Are you going to turn your back on fate?"

"That's exactly what I've spent my adult life doing." Anything to not become a statistic. Protecting herself. By denying herself. Never needing anyone no matter how much she was needed.

"You accepted our offer because it was an easy way out, is that it? We whisked you away from New York," Cozumel said. "And from seeing it through with Jackson?"

"Mi amor," Luis said to Cozumel, "maybe I think we made the wrong decision to keep Esme for ourselves. We're not going to stand in the way of Cupid."

"Wait a minute here. I didn't leave him. He's the one who cut it off." As always, she was the reed that had to bend with the wind. Always the teacher, always the forgiver. She'd had enough of that.

Yet she did need him. He gave her herself. He was the missing piece for her to become whole. By his side, she could soar. They'd be there to catch each other if the flight wasn't smooth.

Luis came away from the stove to give Cozumel a hug and kissed her face a dozen times. "When Cozumel and I found out we weren't able to become pregnant, we decided to share all the wisdom we'd gained in our own struggles by making the spa our baby that we created together."

"I predict you and Jackson will have many babies besides the Sher, although that's a good place to start," Cozumel said. "I have a few other people I can talk to about Itza's job. Go back to New York."

"It's too late."

"It's never too late."

"We don't need you hanging around like a sad yard dog," Luis added. The three of them smiled.

Cozumel was right to feel it in her bones. Esme did, too. Her body didn't align without Jackson; she was off kilter. Hiding from him was not the solution. And Cozumel and Luis had seen their vision come to fruition here. Esme couldn't be happy tagging on to their dream. She was finally ready to see her own. She'd gratefully take all Jackson had to give her.

Within hours, she was standing in front of the spa's tiled fountain with a suitcase by her side, just as she'd arrived. She gave Cozumel and Luis a final wave as she got into the car that would take her to the airport. The couple put their arms around each other as they watched her go.

Love conquers all was only a phrase Esme had heard. She needed that promise to be good to its words.

Once Jackson stepped off of the airplane and inhaled that fresh smell, he felt better. It was as if the flight took one hundred hours, so desperate was he to get back to Mexico and claim what was his. He didn't mean that to sound like a caveman but he wanted to try the image on for size. He liked the fit very much. His and hers.

Ah, Oaxaca. Where bliss had taken flight. The frozen kisses of Stockholm started it and

Thailand's beautiful journey was the end but the warm skies of Oaxaca were unimaginably romantic. It was here he'd started to believe that everything was possible. Until he let the monsters wreck it. Just a few weeks ago, in the quiet night with Esme, he'd started to think he could throw his past into the firepit and watch it burn to ash. Turned out, he wasn't able to. That was then. This was now. With no chance of not getting it right. Esme was his. He was hers. End of story, or should he say beginning.

The airport was just as he remembered it, as was a particular smell of the terrain. He could recognize it with his eyes closed. He fantasized returning to visit here with Esme. That was if Cozumel and Luis forgave him for the tumult he was about to cause. Maybe this could become a special hideaway for him and Esme. Maybe they'd bring their children. Maybe their grandchildren. He enjoyed that thought. He wanted all of that old and gray stuff with her.

He carried his small bag through the terminal. He hadn't packed much because they weren't staying long this time. He got a partial view of a woman walking toward him, her face obscured by other people. He craned his neck to see more. About her height and the same bouncy brown hair with golden highlights. Was he hallucinating?

Some people veered left or right so much that a space opened and they caught sight of each other.

"Jackson?" she exclaimed once he came into focus.

A rosy wash softly poured over him to hear her say his name. All was not lost. He hoped. "It is, my love." My love.

"What are you doing at the airport?"

"I came for you."

"You what?" She stopped a few feet before reaching him. Maybe to stake her own ground before entering his.

"I made a horrible mistake. I came to correct it." He advanced a few steps. "I can't live without you. And I won't."

"How was the Sher's reopening?" Oh, she needed to divert the topic. Okay, he had plenty of time to get everything said.

"The dedication plaque turned out beautiful. I can't wait for you to see it. I did what I intended to do. In my small way I made a peace offering for all the disappointment I caused my parents."

Then Esme took steps toward him, closing the gap. "You didn't disappoint them. Livia did. We've got to get you to forgive yourself."

"In any case, the Sher is ours now. We're going to grow it from seed like two gardeners in the field." Her face lit up. "What did that make you think of?"

"Oh, just something Cozumel said about the Sher being our baby."

"Esme, in almost losing you I realized how much I am ready for you. If you'll have me, stumbles and wobbles and all." Finally, she stepped close enough that he could almost feel her. His breath quickened. "Wait a minute, though. Where are you going? Why are you at the airport?"

People passed by them, coming and going in every direction. A man walked through an exit gate and what looked to be his family rushed to hug him, the four of them running into a tight embrace. A couple deplaned holding hands, the woman wearing a sash that read Bride, both with big smiles on their faces. One young woman dropped her purse and its contents spilled onto the floor. A man about her age dropped to his knees to help her gather up her things and she smiled up at him. Jackson flashed back to the first day he'd returned to the Sher and Esme had been so kind with an elderly woman whose belongings had fallen out of her purse the same way. Lovers parted, after kissing until one had to hurry through the boarding gate. Tour groups and sports teams juggled carry-ons along with their coffees and electronics. Esme and Jackson were two people in the middle of the world, making rotations around the sun, most everyone doing their best.

"I was heading back to you, Jackson."

"I'm capable of evolving."

"We already decided…our starting place is total distrust." They both smirked.

"I'm further than that now."

"Are you?"

"You'll love the new version of me." He touched his own face with his fingers. "Look how I have a skin care regime now. I'm deep breathing. Kenji on our staff is fabulous at shiatsu massage. And I'm seeing a psychologist."

She brought her hand over his on his cheek. Explosions of joy went off inside of him. "I love you."

He wrapped his arms around her, lifted her up and spun her in a circle. "I love you."

When he put her down, she looped her arm through his. "Come on." They headed in the same direction, like they always would. "I heard about this job in New York I just have to have."

* * * * *

If you enjoyed this story,
check out these other great reads
from Andrea Bolter

Pretend Honeymoon with the Best Man
Adventure with a Secret Prince

Available now!